THE BELL-RINGER OF ANGEL'S

and Other Stories

BRET HARTE

1st WORLD
LIBRARY
Literary Society

The Bell-Ringer of Angel's and Other Stories

Bret Harte

© 1st World Library, 2007
PO Box 2211
Fairfield, IA 52556
www.1stworldlibrary.com
First Edition

LCCN: 2007927765

Softcover ISBN: 978-1-4218-4507-4
Hardcover ISBN: 978-1-4218-4423-7
eBook ISBN: 978-1-4218-4591-3

Purchase *"The Bell-Ringer of Angel's and Other Stories"*
as a traditional bound book at:
www.1stWorldLibrary.com/purchase.asp?ISBN=978-1-4218-4507-4

1st World Library is a literary, educational organization
dedicated to:

- Creating a free internet library of downloadable ebooks

- Hosting writing competitions and offering book
  publishing scholarships.

Interested in more 1st World Library books?
contact: literacy@1stworldlibrary.com
Check us out at: www.1stworldlibrary.com

1ˢᵗ World Library Literary Society

Giving Back to the World

"If you want to work on the core problem, it's early school literacy."

- James Barksdale, former CEO of Netscape

"No skill is more crucial to the future of a child, or to a democratic and prosperous society, than literacy."

- Los Angeles Times

"Literacy... means far more than learning how to read and write... The aim is to transmit... knowledge and promote social participation."

- UNESCO

"Literacy is not a luxury, it is a right and a responsibility. If our world is to meet the challenges of the twenty-first century we must harness the energy and creativity of all our citizens."

- President Bill Clinton

"Parents should be encouraged to read to their children, and teachers should be equipped with all available techniques for teaching literacy, so the varying needs and capacities of individual kids can be taken into account."

- Hugh Mackay

CONTENTS

THE BELL-RINGER OF ANGEL'S 7

JOHNNYBOY 48

YOUNG ROBIN GRAY 64

THE SHERIFF OF SISKYOU 95

A ROSE OF GLENBOGIE 124

THE MYSTERY OF THE HACIENDA.............. 151

CHU CHU 196

MY FIRST BOOK................................... 224

THE BELL-RINGER OF ANGEL'S

CHAPTER I

Where the North Fork of the Stanislaus River begins to lose its youthful grace, vigor, and agility, and broadens more maturely into the plain, there is a little promontory which at certain high stages of water lies like a small island in the stream. To the strongly-marked heroics of Sierran landscape it contrasts a singular, pastoral calm. White and gray mosses from the overhanging rocks and feathery alders trail their filaments in its slow current, and between the woodland openings there are glimpses of vivid velvet sward, even at times when the wild oats and "wire-grasses" of the plains are already yellowing. The placid river, unstained at this point by mining sluices or mill drift, runs clear under its contemplative shadows. Originally the camping-ground of a Digger Chief, it passed from his tenancy with the American rifle bullet that terminated his career. The pioneer who thus succeeded to its attractive calm gave way in turn to a well-directed shot from the revolver of a quartz-prospector, equally impressed with the charm of its restful tranquillity. How long he might have enjoyed its riparian seclusion is not known. A sudden rise of the river one March night quietly removed him, together with the overhanging post oak beneath which he was profoundly but unconsciously meditating. The demijohn of whiskey was picked up further down. But no other suggestion of these successive evictions was ever visible in the reposeful serenity of the spot.

It was later occupied, and a cabin built upon the spot, by one Alexander McGee, better known as "the Bell-ringer of Angel's." This euphonious title, which might have suggested a consistently peaceful occupation, however, referred to his accuracy of aim at a mechanical target, where the piercing of the bull's eye was celebrated by the stroke of a bell. It is probable that this singular proficiency kept his investment of that gentle seclusion unchallenged. At all events it was uninvaded. He shared it only with the birds. Perhaps some suggestion of nest building may have been in his mind, for one pleasant spring morning he brought hither a wife. It was his OWN; and in this way he may be said to have introduced that morality which is supposed to be the accompaniment and reflection of pastoral life. Mrs. McGee's red petticoat was sometimes seen through the trees—a cheerful bit of color. Mrs. McGee's red cheeks, plump little figure, beribboned hat and brown, still-girlish braids were often seen at sunset on the river bank, in company with her husband, who seemed to be pleased with the discreet and distant admiration that followed them. Strolling under the bland shadows of the cotton-woods, by the fading gold of the river, he doubtless felt that peace which the mere world cannot give, and which fades not away before the clear, accurate eye of the perfect marksman.

Their nearest neighbors were the two brothers Wayne, who took up a claim, and built themselves a cabin on the river bank near the promontory. Quiet, simple men, susp-ected somewhat of psalm-singing, and undue retirement on Sundays, they attracted but little attention. But when, through some original conception or pain-staking deliberation, they turned the current of the river so as to restrict the overflow between the promontory and the river bank, disclosing an auriferous "bar" of inconceivable richness, and establishing their theory that it was really the former channel of the river, choked and diverted though ages of alluvial drift, they may be said to have changed, also, the fortunes of the little settlement. Popular feeling and the new prosperity which dawned upon the miners recognized the two brothers by giving the name of Wayne's Bar to the infant settlement and its post-office. The peaceful promontory, although made easier of access, still preserved its calm seclusion, and pretty Mrs. McGee could contemplate through the leaves of her bower the work going on at its base, herself unseen. Nevertheless, this Arcadian retreat was being slowly and surely invested; more than that, the character of its surroundings was altered, and the complexion of the river had changed. The Wayne engines on the point above had turned the drift and debris into the current that now thickened and ran yellow around the wooded shore. The fringes of this Eden were already tainted with the color of gold.

It is doubtful, however, if Mrs. McGee was much affected by this sentimental reflection, and her husband, in a manner, lent himself to the desecration of his exclusive domain by accepting a claim along the shore—tendered by the conscientious Waynes in compensation for restricting the approach to the promontory—and thus participated in the fortunes of the Bar. Mrs. McGee amused herself by watching from her eyrie, with a presumably childish interest, the operations of the red-shirted brothers on the Bar; her husband, however, always accompanying her when she crossed the Bar to the bank. Some two or three other women—wives of miners—had joined the camp, but it was evident that McGee was as little inclined to intrust his wife to their companionship as to that of their husbands. An opinion obtained that McGee, being an old resident, with alleged high connec-tions in Angel's, was inclined to be aristocratic and exclusive.

Meantime, the two brothers who had founded the fortunes of the Bar were accorded an equally high position, with an equal amount of reserve. Their ways were decidedly not those of the other miners, and were as efficacious in keeping them from familiar advances as the reputation of Mr. McGee was in isolating his wife. Madison Wayne, the elder, was tall, well-knit and spare, reticent in speech and slow in deduction; his brother, Arthur, was of rounder outline, but smaller and of a more delicate and perhaps a more impressible nature. It was believed by some that it was within the range of possibility that Arthur would yet be seen "taking his cocktail like a white man," or "dropping his scads" at draw poker. At present, however, they seemed content to spend their evenings in their own cabin, and their Sundays at a grim Presbyterian tabernacle in the next town, to which they walked ten miles, where, it was currently believed, "hell fire was ladled out free," and "infants damned for nothing." When they did not go to meeting it was also believed that the minister came to them, until it was ascertained that the sound of sacred recitation overheard in their cabin was simply Madison Wayne reading the Bible to his younger brother. McGee is said to have stopped on one of these occasions—unacc-ompanied by his wife—before their cabin, moving away afterwards with more than his usual placid contentment.

It was about eleven o'clock one morning, and Madison Wayne was at work alone on the Bar. Clad in a dark gray jersey and white duck trousers rolled up over high india-rubber boots, he looked not unlike a peaceful fisherman digging stakes for his nets, as he labored in the ooze and gravel of the still half-reclaimed river bed. He was far out on the Bar, within a stone's throw of the promontory. Suddenly his quick ear caught an unfamiliar cry and splash. Looking up hastily, he saw Mrs. McGee's red petticoat in the water under the singularly agitated boughs of an overhanging tree. Madison Wayne ran to the bank, threw off his heavy boots, and sprang into the stream. A few strokes brought him to Mrs. McGee's petticoat, which, as he had wisely surmised, contained Mrs. McGee, who was still clinging to a branch of the tree. Grasping her waist with one hand and the branch with the other, he obtained a foothold on the bank, and dragged her ashore. A moment later they both stood erect and dripping at the foot of the tree.

"Well?" said the lady.

Wayne glanced around their seclusion with his habitual caution, slightly knit his brows perplexedly, and said: "You fell in?"

"I didn't do nothin' of the sort. I JUMPED in."

Wayne again looked around him, as if expecting her companion, and squeezed the water out of his thick hair. "Jumped in?" he repeated slowly. "What for?"

"To make you come over here, Mad Wayne," she said, with a quick laugh, putting her arms akimbo.

They stood looking at each other, dripping like two river gods. Like them, also, Wayne had apparently ignored the fact that his trousers were rolled up above his bare knees, and Mrs. McGee that her red petticoat clung closely to her rather pretty figure. But he quickly recovered himself.

"You had better go in and change your clothes," he said, with grave concern. "You'll take cold."

She only shook herself disdainfully. "I'm all right," she said; "but YOU, Mad Wayne, what do you mean by not speaking to me—not knowing me? You can't say that I've changed like that." She passed her hand down her long dripping braids as if to press the water from them, and yet with a half-coquettish suggestion in the act.

Something struggled up into the man's face which was not there before. There was a new light in his grave eyes. "You look the same," he said slowly; "but you are married —you have a husband."

"You think that changes a girl?" she said, with a laugh "That's where all you men slip up! You're afraid of his rifle—THAT'S the change that bothers you, Mad."

"You know I care little for carnal weapons," he said quietly. She DID know it; but it is the privilege of the sex to invent its facts and then to graciously abandon them as if they were only arguments. "Then why do you keep off from me? Why do you look the other way when I pass?" she said quickly.

"Because you are married," he said slowly.

She again shook the water from her like a Newfoundland dog. "That's it. You're mad because I got married. You're mad because I wouldn't marry you and your church over on the cross roads, and sing hymns with you and become SISTER Wayne. You wanted me to give up dancing and buggy ridin' Sundays—and you're just mad because I didn't. Yes, mad—just mean, baby mad, Mr. Maddy Wayne, for all your CHRISTIAN resignation! That's what's the matter with you." Yet she looked very pretty and piquant in her small spitefulness, which was still so general and superficial that she seemed to shake it out of her wet petticoats in a vicious flap that disclosed her neat ankles.

"You preferred McGee to me," he said grimly. "I didn't blame you."

"Who said I PREFERRED him?" she retorted quickly. "Much you know!" Then, with swift feminine abandonment of her position, she added, with a little laugh, "It's all the same whether you're guarded with a rifle or a Church Presbytery, only"—

"Only what?" said Madison earnestly.

"There's men who'd risk being SHOT for a girl, that couldn't stand psalm-singin' palaver."

The quick expression of pain that passed over his hard, dark face seemed only to heighten her pretty mischievousness. But he simply glanced again around the solitude, passed his hand over his wet sleeve, and said, "I must go now; your husband wouldn't like me being here."

"He's workin' in the claim,—the claim YOU gave him," said Mrs. McGee, with cheerful malice. "Wonder what he'd say if he knew it was given to him by the man who used to spark his wife only two years ago? How does that suit your Christian conscience, Mad?"

"I should have told him, had I not believed that everything was over between us, or that it was possible that you and me should ever meet again," he returned, in a tone so measured that the girl seemed to hear the ring of the conventicle in it.

"Should you, BROTHER Wayne?" she said, imitating him. "Well, let me tell you that you are the one man on the Bar that Sandy has taken a fancy to."

Madison's sallow cheek colored a little, but he did not speak.

"Well!" continued Mrs. McGee impatiently. "I don't believe he'd object to your comin' here to see me—if you cared."

"But I wouldn't care to come, unless he first knew that I had been once engaged to you," said Madison gravely.

"Perhaps he might not think as much of that as you do," retorted the woman pertly. "Every one isn't as straitlaced as you, and every girl has had one or two engagements. But do as you like—stay at home if you want to, and sing psalms and read the Scriptures to that younger brother of yours! All the same, I'm thinkin' he'd rather be out with the boys."

"My brother is God-fearing and conscientious," said Madison quickly. "You do not know him. You have never seen him."

"No," said Mrs. McGee shortly. She then gave a little shiver (that was, however, half simulated) in her wet garments, and added: "ONE saint was enough for me; I couldn't stand the whole church, Mad."

"You are catching cold," he said quickly, his whole face brightening with a sudden tenderness that seemed to transfigure the dark features. "I am keeping you here when you should be changing your clothes. Go, I beg you, at once."

She stood still provokingly, with an affectation of wiping her arms and shoulders and sopping her wet dress with clusters of moss.

"Go, please do—Safie, please!"

"Ah!"—she drew a quick, triumphant breath. "Then you'll come again to see me, Mad?"

"Yes," he said slowly, and even more gravely than before.

"But you must let me show you the way out—round under those trees—where no one can see you come." She held out her hand.

"I'll go the way I came," he said quietly, swinging himself silently from the nearest bough into the stream. And before she could utter a protest he was striking out as silently, hand over hand, across the current.

CHAPTER II

A week later Madison Wayne was seated alone in his cabin. His supper table had just been cleared by his Chinese coolie, as it was getting late, and the setting sun, which for half an hour had been persistently making a vivid beacon of his windows for the benefit of wayfarers along the river bank, had at last sunk behind the cottonwoods. His head was resting on his hand; the book he had been reading when the light faded was lying open on the table before him. In this attitude he became aware of a hesitating step on the gravel outside his open door. He had been so absorbed that the approach of any figure along the only highway—the river bank—had escaped his observation. Looking up, he discovered that Mr. Alexander McGee was standing in the doorway, his hand resting lightly on the jamb. A sudden color suffused Wayne's cheek; his hand reached for his book, which he drew towards him hurriedly, yet half automatically, as he might have grasped some defensive weapon.

The Bell-ringer of Angel's noticed the act, but not the blush, and nodded approvingly. "Don't let me disturb ye. I was only meanderin' by and reckoned I'd say 'How do?' in passin'." He leaned gently back against the door-post, to do which comfortably he was first obliged to shift the revolver on his hip. The sight of the weapon brought a slight contraction to the brows of Wayne, but he gravely said: "Won't you come in?"

"It ain't your prayin' time?" said McGee politely.

"No."

"Nor you ain't gettin' up lessons outer the Book?" he

Bret Harte

continued thoughtfully.

"No."

"Cos it don't seem, so to speak, you see, the square thing to be botherin' a man when he might be doin' suthin' else, don't you see? You understand what I mean?"

It was his known peculiarity that he always seemed to be suffering from an inability to lucid expression, and the fear of being misunderstood in regard to the most patent or equally the most unimportant details of his speech. All of which, however, was in very remarkable contrast to his perfectly clear and penetrating eyes.

Wayne gravely assured him that he was not interrupting him in any way.

"I often thought—that is, I had an idea, you understand what I mean—of stoppin' in passing. You and me, you see, are sorter alike; we don't seem to jibe in with the gin'ral gait o' the camp. You understand what I mean? We ain't in the game, eh? You see what I'm after?"

Madison Wayne glanced half mechanically at McGee's revolver. McGee's clear eyes at once took in the glance.

"That's it! You understand? You with them books of yours, and me with my shootin' iron—we're sort o' different from the rest, and ought to be kinder like partners. You understand what I mean? We keep this camp in check. We hold a full hand, and don't stand no bluffing."

"If you mean there is some effect in Christian example and the life of a God-fearing man"—began Madison gravely.

"That's it! God-fearin' or revolver-fearin', it amounts to the same when you come down to the hard pan and bedrock," interrupted McGee. "I ain't expectin' you to think much of my style, but I go a heap on yours, even if I can't play your game. And I sez to my wife, 'Safie'—her that trots around with me sometimes—I sez, 'Safie, I oughter know that man, and shall. And I WANT YOU to know him.' Hol' on," he added quickly, as Madison rose with a flushed face and a perturbed gesture. "Ye don't understand! I see wot's in your mind—don't you see? When I married my wife and brought her down here, knowin' this yer camp, I sez: 'No flirtin', no foolin', no philanderin' here, my dear! You're young and don't know the ways o' men. The first man I see you talking with, I shoot. You needn't fear, my dear, for accidents. I kin shoot all round you, under your arm, across your shoulders, over your head and between your fingers, my dear, and never start skin or fringe or ruffle. But I don't miss HIM. You sorter understand what I mean,' sez I,'so don't!' Ye noticed how my wife is respected, Mr. Wayne? Queen Victoria sittin' on her throne ain't in it with my Safie. But when I see YOU not herdin' with that cattle, never liftin' your eyes to me or Safie as we pass, never hangin' round the saloons and jokin', nor winkin', nor slingin' muddy stories about women, but prayin' and readin' Scripter stories, here along with your brother, I sez to myself, I sez, 'Sandy, ye kin take off your revolver and hang up your shot gun when HE'S around. For 'twixt HIM and your wife ain't no revolver, but the fear of God and hell and damnation and the world to come!' You understand what I mean, don't ye? Ye sorter follow my lead, eh? Ye can see what I'm shootin' round, don't ye? So I want you to come up neighborly like, and drop in to see my wife."

Madison Wayne's face became set and hard again, but he

advanced towards McGee with the book against his breast, and his finger between the leaves. "I already know your wife, Mr. McGee! I saw her before YOU ever met her. I was engaged to her; I loved her, and—as far as man may love the wife of another and keep the commands of this book—I love her still!"

To his surprise, McGee, whose calm eyes had never dimmed or blenched, after regarding him curiously, took the volume from him, laid it on the table, opened it, turned its leaves critically, said earnestly, "That's the law here, is it?" and then held out his hand.

"Shake!"

Madison Wayne hesitated—and then grasped his hand.

"Ef I had known this," continued McGee, "I reckon I wouldn't have been so hard on Safie and so partikler. She's better than I took her for—havin' had you for a beau! You understand what I mean. You follow me— don't ye? I allus kinder wondered why she took me, but sens you've told me that YOU used to spark her, in your God-fearin' way, I reckon it kinder prepared her for ME. You understand? Now you come up, won't ye?"

"I will call some evening with my brother," said Wayne embarrassedly.

"With which?" demanded McGee.

"My brother Arthur. We usually spend the evenings together."

McGee paused, leaned against the doorpost, and, fixing his clear eyes on Wayne, said: "Ef it's all the same to you,

I'd rather you did not bring him. You understand what I mean? You follow me; no other man but you and me. I ain't sayin' anything agin' your brother, but you see how it is, don't you? Just me and you."

"Very well, I will come," said Wayne gloomily. But as McGee backed out of the door, he followed him, hesitatingly. Then, with an effort he seemed to recover himself, and said almost harshly: "I ought to tell you another thing—that I have seen and spoken to Mrs. McGee since she came to the Bar. She fell into the water last week, and I swam out and dragged her ashore. We talked and spoke of the past."

"She fell in," echoed McGee.

Wayne hesitated; then a murky blush came into his face as he slowly repeated, "She FELL in."

McGee's eyes only brightened. "I have been too hard on her. She might have drowned ef you hadn't took risks. You see? You understand what I mean? And she never let out anything about it—and never boasted o' YOU helpin' her out. All right—you'll come along and see her agin'." He turned and walked cheerfully away.

Wayne re-entered the cabin. He sat for a long time by the window until the stars came out above the river, and another star, with which he had been long familiar, took its place apparently in the heart of the wooded crest of the little promontory. Then the fringing woods on the opposite shore became a dark level line across the landscape, and the color seemed to fade out of the moist shining gravel before his cabin. Presently the silhouette of his dark face disappeared from the window, and Mr. McGee might have been gratified to know that he had slipped to his knees before the chair whereon he had been sitting, and that his head was bowed before it on his clasped hands. In a little while he rose again, and, dragging a battened old portmanteau from the corner, took out a number of letters tied up in a package, with which, from time to time, he slowly fed the flame that flickered on his hearth. In this way the windows of the cabin at times sprang into light, making a somewhat confusing beacon for the somewhat confused Arthur Wayne, who was returning from a visit to Angel's, and who had fallen into that slightly morose and irritated state which follows excessive hilarity, and is also apt to indicate moral misgivings.

But the last letter was burnt and the cabin quite dark when he entered. His brother was sitting by the slowly dying fire, and he trusted that in that uncertain light any observation of his expression or manner—of which he himself was uneasily conscious—would pass unheeded.

"You are late," said Madison gravely.

At which his brother rashly assumed the aggressive. He was no later than the others, and if the Rogers boys were good enough to walk with him for company he couldn't run ahead of them just because his brother was waiting! He didn't want any supper, he had something at the Cross Roads with the others. Yes! WHISKEY, if he wanted to know. People couldn't keep coffee and temperance drinks just to please him and his brother, and he wasn't goin' to insult the others by standing aloof. Anyhow, he had never taken the pledge, and as long as he hadn't he couldn't see why he should refuse a single glass. As it was, everybody said he was a milksop, and a tender-foot, and he was just sick of it.

Madison rose and lit a candle and held it up before his brother's face. It was a handsome, youthful face that looked into his, flushed with the excitement of novel experiences and perhaps a more material stimulation. The little silken moustache was ostentatiously curled, the brown curls were redolent of bear's grease. Yet there was a certain boyish timidity and nervousness in the defiance of his blue eyes that momentarily touched the elder brother.

"I've been too hand with him," he said to himself, half consciously recalling what McGee had said of Safie. He put the candle down, laid his hand gently on Arthur's shoulder, and said, with a certain cautious tenderness, "Come, Arty, sit down and tell me all about it."

Whereupon the mercurial Arthur, not only relieved of his nervousness but of his previous ethical doubts and remorse, became gay and voluble. He had finished his purchases at Angel's, and the storekeeper had introduced him to Colonel Starbottle, of Kentucky, as one of "the Waynes who had made Wayne's Bar famous." Colonel Starbottle had said in his pompous fashion—yet he was not such a bad fellow, after all—that the Waynes ought to be represented in the Councils of the State, and that he, Starbottle, would be proud to nominate Madison for the next Legislature and run him, too. "And you know, really, Mad, if you mixed a little more with folks, and they weren't—well, sorter AFRAID of you—you could do it. Why, I've made a heap o' friends over there, just by goin' round a little, and one of old Selvedge's girls—the storekeeper, you know—said from what she'd heard of us, she always thought I was about fifty, and turned up the whites of my eyes instead of the ends of my moustache! She's mighty smart! Then the Postmaster has got his wife and three daughters out from the States, and they've asked me to come over to their church festival next week. It isn't our church, of course, but I suppose it's all right."

This and much more with the volubility of relieved feelings. When he stopped, out of breath, Madison said, "I have had a visitor since you left—Mr. McGee."

"And his wife?" asked Arthur quickly. Madison flushed slightly. "No; but he asked me to go and see her."

"That's HER doin', then," returned Arthur, with a laugh. "She's always lookin' round the corners of her eyes at me when she passes. Why, John Rogers was joking me about her only yesterday, and said McGee would blow a hole through me some of these days if I didn't look out! Of course," he added, affectedly curling his moustache, "that's nonsense! But you know how they talk, and she's too pretty for that fellow McGee."

"She has found a careful helpmeet in her husband," said Madison sternly, "and it's neither seemly nor Christian in you, Arthur, to repeat the idle, profane gossip of the Bar. I knew her before her marriage, and if she was not a professing Christian, she was, and is, a pure, good woman! Let us have no more of this."

Whether impressed by the tone of his brother's voice, or only affected by his own mercurial nature, Arthur changed the subject to further voluble reminiscences of his trip to Angel's. Yet he did not seem embarrassed nor disconcerted when his brother, in the midst of his speech, placed the candle and the Bible on the table, with two chairs before it. He listened to Madison's monotonous reading of the evening exercise with equally monotonous respect. Then they both arose, without looking at each other, but with equally set and stolid faces, and knelt down before their respective chairs, clasping the back with both hands, and occasionally drawing the hard, wooden frames against their breasts convulsively, as if it were a penitential act. It was the elder brother who that night prayed aloud. It was his voice that rose higher by degrees above the low roof and encompassing walls, the level river camp lights that trembled through the window, the dark belt of riverside trees, and the light on the promontory's crest—up to the tranquil, passionless stars themselves.

With those confidences to his Maker this chronicle does not lie—obtrusive and ostentatious though they were in tone and attitude. Enough that they were a general arraignment of humanity, the Bar, himself, and his brother, and indeed much that the same Maker had created and permitted. That through this hopeless denunciation still lingered some human feeling and tenderness might have been shown by the fact that at its close his hands trembled and his face was bedewed by tears. And his brother was so deeply affected that he resolved hereafter to avoid all evening prayers.

CHAPTER III

It was a week later that Madison Wayne and Mr. McGee were seen, to the astonishment of the Bar, leisurely walking together in the direction of the promontory. Here they disappeared, entering a damp fringe of willows and laurels that seemed to mark its limits, and gradually ascending some thickly-wooded trail, until they reached its crest, which, to Madison's surprise, was cleared and open, and showed an acre or two of rude cultivation. Here, too, stood the McGees' conjugal home—a small, four-roomed house, but so peculiar and foreign in aspect that it at once challenged even Madison's abstracted attention. It was a tiny Swiss chalet, built in sections, and originally packed in cases, one of the early importations from Europe to California after the gold discovery, when the country was supposed to be a woodless wilderness. Mr. McGee explained, with his usual laborious care, how he had bought it at Marysville, not only for its picturesqueness, but because in its unsuggestive packing-cases it offered no indication to the curious miners, and could be put up by himself and a single uncommunicative Chinaman, without any one else being aware of its existence. There was, indeed, something quaint in this fragment of Old World handicraft, with its smooth-jointed paneling, in two colors, its little lozenge fretwork, its lapped roof, overhanging eaves, and miniature gallery. Inartistic as Madison was—like most men of rigidly rectangular mind and principle—and accustomed to the bleak and economic sufficiency of the Californian miner's cabin, he was touched strangely by its novel grace and freshness. It reminded him of HER; he had a new respect for this rough, sinful man who had thus idealized his wife in her dwelling. Already a few Madeira vines and a Cherokee rose clambered up the gallery. And here Mrs.

McGee was sitting.

In the face that she turned upon the two men Madison could see that she was not expecting them, and even in the slight curiosity with which she glanced at her husband, that evidently he had said nothing of his previous visit or invitation. And this conviction became certainty at Mr. McGee's first words.

"I've brought you an ole friend, Safie. He used to spark ye once at Angel's afore my time—he told me so; he picked ye outer the water here—he told me that, too. Ye mind that I said afore that he was the only man I wanted ter know; I reckon now it seems the square thing that he should be the one man YOU wanted ter know, too. You understand what I mean—you follow me, don't you?"

Whether or not Mrs. McGee DID follow him, she exhibited neither concern, solicitude, nor the least embarrassment. An experienced lover might have augured ill from this total absence of self-consciousness. But Madison was not an experienced lover. He accepted her amused smile as a recognition of his feelings, trembled at the touch of her cool hands, as if it had been a warm pressure, and scarcely dared to meet her maliciously laughing eyes. When he had followed Mr. McGee to the little gallery, the previous occupation of Mrs. McGee when they arrived was explained. From that slight elevation there was a perfect view over the whole landscape and river below; the Bar stretched out as a map at her feet; in that clear, transparent air she could see every movement and gesture of Wayne's brother, all unconscious of that surveillance, at work on the Bar. For an instant Madison's sallow cheek reddened, he knew not why; a remorseful feeling that he ought to be there with Arthur came over him. Mrs. McGee's voice seemed to answer his thought. "You can see everything that's going on down there without being seen yourself. It's good fun for me sometimes. The other day I saw that young Carpenter hanging round Mrs. Rogers's cabin in the bush when old Rogers was away. And I saw her creep out and join him, never thinking any one could see her!"

She laughed, seeking Madison's averted eyes, yet scarcely noticing his suddenly contracted brows. Mr. McGee alone responded.

"That's why," he said, explanatorily, to Madison, "I don't allow to have my Safie go round with those women. Not as I ever see anything o' that sort goin' on, or keer to look, but on gin'ral principles. You understand what I mean."

"That's your brother over there, isn't it?" said Mrs. McGee, turning to Madison and calmly ignoring her husband's explanation, as she indicated the distant Arthur. "Why didn't you bring him along with you?"

Madison hesitated, and looked at McGee. "He wasn't asked," said that gentleman cheerfully. "One's company, two's none! You don't know him, my dear; and this yer ain't a gin'ral invitation to the Bar. You follow me?"

To this Mrs. McGee made no comment, but proceeded to show Madison over the little cottage. Yet in a narrow passage she managed to touch his hand, lingered to let her husband precede them from one room to another, and once or twice looked meaningly into his eyes over McGee's shoulder. Disconcerted and embarrassed, he tried to utter a few commonplaces, but so constrainedly that even McGee presently noticed it. And the result was still more embarrassing.

"Look yer," he said, suddenly turning to them both. "I reckon as how you two wanter talk over old times, and I'll just meander over to the claim, and do a spell o' work. Don't mind ME. And if HE"—indicating Madison with his finger—"gets on ter religion, don't you mind him. It won't hurt you, Safie,—no more nor my revolver,—but it's pow'ful persuadin', and you understand me? You follow me? Well, so long!"

He turned away quickly, and was presently lost among the trees. For an instant the embarrassed Madison thought of following him; but he was confronted by Mrs. McGee's wicked eyes and smiling face between him and the door. Composing herself, however, with a simulation of perfect gravity she pointed to a chair.

"Sit down, Brother Wayne. If you're going to convert me, it may take some time, you know, and you might as well make yourself comfortable. As for me, I'll take the anxious bench." She laughed with a certain girlishness, which he well remembered, and leaped to a sitting posture on the table with her hands on her knees, swinging her smart shoes backwards and forwards below it.

Madison looked at her in hopeless silence, with a pale, disturbed face and shining eyes.

"Or, if you want to talk as we used to talk, Mad, when we sat on the front steps at Angel's and pa and ma went inside to give us a show, ye can hop up alongside o' me." She made a feint of gathering her skirts beside her.

"Safie!" broke out the unfortunate man, in a tone that seemed to increase in formal solemnity with his manifest agitation, "this is impossible. The laws of God that have joined you and this man"—

"Oh, it's the prayer-meeting, is it?" said Safie, settling her skirts again, with affected resignation. "Go on."

"Listen, Safie," said Madison, turning despairingly towards her. "Let us for His sake, let us for the sake of our dear blessed past, talk together earnestly and prayerfully. Let us take this time to root out of our feeble hearts all yearnings that are not prompted by Him—yearnings that your union with this man makes impossible and sinful. Let us for the sake of the past take counsel of each other, even as brother and sister."

"Sister McGee!" she interrupted mockingly. "It wasn't as brother and sister you made love to me at Angel's."

"No! I loved you then, and would have made you my wife."

"And you don't love me any more," she said, audaciously darting a wicked look into his eyes, "only because I didn't marry you? And you think that Christian?"

"You know I love you as I have loved you always," he said passionately.

"Hush!" she said mockingly; "suppose he should hear you."

"He knows it!" said Madison bitterly. "I told him all!"

She stared at him fixedly.

"You have—told—him—that—you STILL love me?" she repeated slowly.

"Yes, or I wouldn't be here now. It was due to him—to

my own conscience."

"And what did he say?"

"He insisted upon my coming, and, as God is my Judge and witness—he seemed satisfied and content."

She drew her pretty lips together with a long whistle, and then leaped from the table. Her face was hard and her eyes were bright as she went to the window and looked out. He followed her timidly.

"Don't touch me," she said, sharply striking away his proffered hand. He turned with a flushed cheek and walked slowly towards the door. Her laugh stopped him.

"Come! I reckon that squeezin' hands ain't no part of your contract with Sandy?" she said, glancing down at her own. "Well, so you're goin'?"

"I only wished to talk seriously and prayerfully with you for a few moments, Safie, and then—to see you no more."

"And how would that suit him," she said dryly, "if he wants your company here? Then, just because you can't convert me and bring me to your ways of thinkin' in one visit, I suppose you think it is Christian-like to run away like this! Or do you suppose that, if you turn tail now, he won't believe that your Christian strength and Christian resignation is all humbug?"

Madison dropped into the chair, put his elbows on the table, and buried his face in his hands. She came a little nearer, and laid her hand lightly on his arm. He made a movement as if to take it, but she withdrew it impatiently.

"Come," she said brusquely; "now you're in for it you must play the game out. He trusts you; if he sees you can't trust yourself, he'll shoot you on sight. That don't frighten you? Well, perhaps this will then! He'll SAY your religion is a sham and you a hypocrite—and everybody will believe him. How do you like that, Brother Wayne? How will that help the Church? Come! You're a pair of cranks together; but he's got the whip-hand of you this time. All you can do is to keep up to his idea of you. Put a bold face on it, and come here as often as you can—the oftener the better; the sooner you'll both get sick of each other—and of ME. That's what you're both after, ain't it? Well! I can tell you now, you needn't either of you be the least afraid of me."

She walked away to the window again, not angrily, but smoothing down the folds of her bright print dress as if she were wiping her hands of her husband and his guest. Something like a very material and man-like sense of shame struggled up through his crust of religion. He stammered, "You don't understand me, Safie."

"Then talk of something I do understand," she said pertly. "Tell me some news of Angel's. Your brother was over there the other day. He made himself quite popular with the young ladies—so I hear from Mrs. Selvedge. You can tell me as we walk along the bank towards Sandy's claim. It's just as well that you should move on now, as it's your FIRST call, and next time you can stop longer." She went to the corner of the room, removed her smart slippers, and put on a pair of walking-shoes, tying them, with her foot on a chair, in a quiet disregard of her visitor's presence; took a brown holland sunbonnet from the wall, clapped it over her browner hair and hanging braids, and tied it under her chin with apparently no sense of coquetry in the act—becoming though it was—and without glancing at him. Alas for Madison's ethics! The torment of her worldly speech and youthful contempt was nothing to this tacit ignoring of the manhood of her lover—this silent acceptance of him as something even lower than her husband. He followed her with a burning cheek and a curious revolting of his whole nature that it is to be feared were scarcely Christian. The willows opened to let them pass and closed behind them.

An hour later Mrs. McGee returned to her leafy bower alone. She took off her sunbonnet, hung it on its nail on the wall, shook down her braids, took off her shoes, stained with the mud of her husband's claim, and put on her slippers. Then she ascended to her eyrie in the little gallery, and gazed smilingly across the sunlit Bar. The two gaunt shadows of her husband and lover, linked like twins, were slowly passing along the river bank on their way to the eclipsing obscurity of the cottonwoods. Below her—almost at her very feet—the unconscious Arthur Wayne was pushing his work on the river bed, far out to the promontory. The sunlight fell upon his vivid scarlet shirt, his bared throat, and head clustering with perspiring curls. The same sunlight fell upon Mrs. McGee's brown head too, and apparently put a wicked fancy inside it. She ran to her bedroom, and returned with a mirror from its wall, and, after some trials in getting the right angle, sent a searching reflection upon the spot where Arthur was at work.

For an instant a diamond flash played around him. Then he lifted his head and turned it curiously towards the crest above him. But the next moment he clapped his hands over his dazzled but now smiling eyes, as Mrs. McGee, secure in her leafy obscurity, fell back and laughed to herself, like a very schoolgirl.

Bret Harte

It was three weeks later, and Madison Wayne was again sitting alone in his cabin. This solitude had become of more frequent occurrence lately, since Arthur had revolted and openly absented himself from his religious devotions for lighter diversions of the Bar. Keenly as Madison felt his defection, he was too much preoccupied with other things to lay much stress upon it, and the sting of Arthur's relapse to worldliness and folly lay in his own consciousness that it was partly his fault. He could not chide his brother when he felt that his own heart was absorbed in his neighbor's wife, and although he had rigidly adhered to his own crude ideas of self-effacement and loyalty to McGee, he had been again and again a visitor at his house. It was true that Mrs. McGee had made this easier by tacitly accepting his conditions of their acquaintanceship, by seeming more natural, by exhibiting a gayety, and at times even a certain gentleness and thoughtfulness of conduct that delighted her husband and astonished her lover. Whether this wonderful change had really been effected by the latter's gloomy theology and still more hopeless ethics, he could not say. She certainly showed no disposition to imitate their formalities, nor seemed to be impressed by them on the rare occasions when he now offered them. Yet she appeared to link the two men together—even physically—as on these occasions when, taking an arm of each, she walked affectionately between them along the river bank promenade, to the great marveling and admiration of the Bar. It was said, however, that Mr. Jack Hamlin, a gambler, at that moment professionally visiting Wayne's Bar, and a great connoisseur of feminine charms and weaknesses, had glanced at them under his handsome lashes, and asked a single question, evidently so amusing to the younger members of the Bar that Madison Wayne knit his brow and Arthur Wayne blushed. Mr. Hamlin took no heed of the elder brother's frown, but paid some slight attention to the color of the younger brother, and even more to a slightly coquettish glance from the pretty Mrs. McGee. Whether or not—as has been ingeniously alleged by some moralists—the light and trifling of either sex are prone to recognize each other by some mysterious instinct, is not a necessary consideration of this chronicle; enough that the fact is recorded.

And yet Madison Wayne should have been satisfied with his work! His sacrifice was accepted; his happy issue from a dangerous situation, and his happy triumph over a more dangerous temptation, was complete and perfect, and even achieved according to his own gloomy theories of redemption and regeneration. Yet he was not happy. The human heart is at times strangely unappeasable. And as he sat that evening in the gathering shadows, the Book which should have yielded him balm and comfort lay unopened in his lap.

A step upon the gravel outside had become too familiar to startle him. It was Mr. McGee lounging into the cabin like a gaunt shadow. It must be admitted that the friendship of these strangely contrasted men, however sincere and sympathetic, was not cheerful. A belief in the thorough wickedness of humanity, kept under only through fear of extreme penalty and punishment, material and spiritual, was not conducive to light and amusing conversation. Their talk was mainly a gloomy chronicle of life at the Bar, which was in itself half an indictment. To-night, Mr. McGee spoke of the advent of Mr. Jack Hamlin, and together they deplored the diversion of the hard-earned gains and valuable time of the Bar through the efforts of that ingenious gentleman. "Not," added McGee cautiously, "but what he can shoot straight enough, and I've heard tell that he don't LIE. That mout and it moutn't be good for your brother who goes around with him considerable, there's different ways of lookin' at that; you understand what I mean? You follow me?" For all that, the conversation seemed to languish this evening, partly through some abstraction on the part of Wayne and partly some hesitation in McGee, who appeared to have a greater fear than usual of not expressing himself plainly. It was quite dark in the cabin when at last, detaching himself from his usual lounging place, the door-post, he walked to the window and leaned, more shadowy than ever, over Wayne's chair. "I want to tell you suthin'," he said slowly, "that I don't want you to misunderstand—you follow me? and that ain't no ways carpin' or criticisin' nor reflectin' on YOU—you understand what I mean? Ever sens you and me had that talk here about you and Safie, and ever sens I got the hang of your ways and your style o' thinkin', I've been as sure of you and her as if I'd been myself trottin' round with you and a revolver. And I'm as sure of you now—you sabe what I mean? you understand? You've done me and her a heap o' good; she's almost another woman sens you took hold of her, and ef you ever want me to stand up and 'testify,' as you call it, in church, Sandy McGee is ready. What I'm tryin' to say to ye is this. Tho' I understand you and your work and your ways—there's other folks ez moutn't—you follow? You understand what I mean? And it's just that I'm coming to. Now las' night, when you and Safie was meanderin' along the lower path by the water, and I kem across you"—

"But," interrupted Madison quickly, "you're mistaken. I wasn't"—

"Hol' on," said McGee, quietly; "I know you got out o' the way without you seein' me or me you, because you didn't know it was me, don't you see? don't you follow? and that's just it! It mout have bin some one from the Bar as seed you instead o' ME. See? That's why you lit out before I could recognize you, and that's why poor Safie was so mighty flustered at first and was for runnin' away until she kem to herself agin. When, of course, she laughed, and agreed you must have mistook me."

"But," gasped Madison quickly, "I WASN'T THERE AT ALL LAST NIGHT."

"What?"

The two men had risen simultaneously and were facing each other. McGee, with a good-natured, half-critical expression, laid his hand on Wayne's shoulder and slightly turned him towards the window, that he might see his face. It seemed to him white and dazed.

"You—wasn't there—last night?" he repeated, with a slow tolerance.

Scarcely a moment elapsed, but the agony of an hour may have thrilled through Wayne's consciousness before he spoke. Then all the blood of his body rushed to his face with his first lie as he stammered, "No! Yes! Of course. I have made a mistake—it WAS I."

"I see—you thought I was riled?" said McGee quietly.

"No; I was thinking it was NIGHT BEFORE LAST! Of course it was last night. I must be getting silly." He essayed a laugh—rare at any time with him—and so forced now that it affected McGee more than his embarrassment. He looked at Wayne thoughtfully, and then said slowly: "I reckon I did come upon you a little too sudden last night, but, you see, I was thinkin' of suthin' else and disremembered you might be there. But I

Bret Harte

wasn't mad—no! no! and I only spoke about it now that you might be more keerful before folks. You follow me? You understand what I mean?"

He turned and walked to the door, when he halted. "You follow me, don't you? It ain't no cussedness o' mine, or want o' trustin', don't you see? Mebbe I oughtened have spoken. I oughter remembered that times this sort o' thing must be rather rough on you and her. You follow me? You understand what I mean? Good-night."

He walked slowly down the path towards the river. Had Madison Wayne been watching him, he would have noticed that his head was bent and his step less free. But Madison Wayne was at that moment sitting rigidly in his chair, nursing, with all the gloomy concentration of a monastic nature, a single terrible suspicion.

CHAPTER IV

Howbeit the sun shone cheerfully over the Bar the next morning and the next; the breath of life and activity was in the air; the settlement never had been more prosperous, and the yield from the opened placers on the drained river-bed that week was enormous. The Brothers Wayne were said to be "rolling in gold." It was thought to be consistent with Madison Wayne's nature that there was no trace of good fortune in his face or manner—rather that he had become more nervous, restless, and gloomy. This was attributed to the joylessness of avarice as contrasted with the spendthrift gayety of the more liberal Arthur, and he was feared and RESPECTED as a miser. His long, solitary walks around the promontory, his incessant watchfulness, his reticence when questioned, were all recognized as the indications of a man whose soul was absorbed in money-getting. The reverence they failed to yield to his religious isolation they were willing to freely accord to his financial abstraction. But Mr. McGee was not so deceived. Overtaking him one day under the fringe of willows, he characteristically chided him with absenting himself from Mrs. McGee and her house since their last interview.

"I reckon you did not harbor malice in your Christianity," he said; "but it looks mighty like ez if ye was throwing off on Safie and me on account of what I said."

In vain Madison gloomily and almost sternly protested.

McGee looked him all over with his clear measuring eye, and for some minutes was singularly silent. At last he said slowly: "I've been thinkin' suthin' o' goin' down to 'Frisco, and I'd be a heap easier in my mind ef you'd promise to look arter Safie now and then."

"You surely are not going to leave her here ALONE?" said Wayne roughly.

"Why not?"

For an instant Wayne hesitated. Then he burst out. "For a hundred reasons! If she ever wanted your protection, before, she surely does now. Do you suppose the Bar is any less heathen or more regenerated than it was when you thought it necessary to guard her with your revolver? Man! It is a hundred times worse than then! The new claims have filled it with spying adventurers—with wolves like Hamlin and his friends—idolaters who would set up Baal and Ashteroth here—and fill your tents with the curses of Sodom!"

Perhaps it was owing to the Scriptural phrasing, perhaps it was from some unusual authority of the man's manner, but a look of approving relief and admiration came into McGee's clear eyes.

"And YOU'RE just the man to tackle 'em," he said, clapping his hand on Wayne's shoulder. "That's your gait —keep it up! But," he added, in a lower voice, "me and my revolver are played out." There was a strangeness in the tone that arrested Wayne's attention. "Yes," continued McGee, stroking his beard slowly, "men like me has their day, and revolvers has theirs; the world turns round and the Bar fills up, and this yer river changes its course—and it's all in the day's work. You understand what I mean— you follow me? And if anything should happen to me— not that it's like to; but it's in the way o' men—I want you to look arter Safie. It ain't every woman ez has two men, ez like and unlike, to guard her. You follow me—you understand what I mean, don't you?" With these words he parted somewhat abruptly from Wayne, turning into the steep path to the promontory crest and leaving his companion lost in gloomy abstraction. The next day Alexander McGee had departed on a business trip to San Francisco.

In his present frame of mind, with his new responsibility and the carrying out of a plan which he had vaguely conceived might remove the terrible idea that had taken possession of him, Madison Wayne was even relieved when his brother also announced his intention of going to Angel's for a few days.

For since his memorable interview with McGee he had been convinced that Safie had been clandestinely visited by some one. Whether it was the thoughtless and momentary indiscretion of a willful woman, or the sequel to some deliberately planned intrigue, did not concern him so much as the falsity of his own position, and the conniving lie by which he had saved her and her lover. That at this crucial moment he had failed to "testify" to guilt and wickedness; that he firmly believed—such is the inordinate vanity of the religious zealot—that he had denied Him in his effort to shield HER; and that he had broken faith with the husband who had entrusted to him the custody of his wife's honor, seemed to him more terrible than her faithlessness. In his first horror he had dreaded to see her, lest her very confession—he knew her reckless frankness towards himself—should reveal to him the extent of his complicity. But since then, and during her husband's absence, he had convinced himself that it was his duty to wrestle and strive with her weak spirit, to implore her to reveal her new intrigue to her husband, and then he would help her to sue for his forgiveness. It was a part of the inconsistency of his religious convictions; in his human passion he was perfectly unselfish, and had already forgiven her the offense against himself. He would see her at once!

But it happened to be a quiet, intense night, with the tremulous opulence of a full moon that threw quivering shafts of light like summer lightning over the blue river, and laid a wonderful carpet of intricate lace along the path that wound through the willows to the crest. There was the dry, stimulating dust and spice of heated pines from below; the languorous odors of syringa; the faint, feminine smell of southernwood, and the infinite mystery of silence. This silence was at times softly broken with the tender inarticulate whisper of falling leaves, broken sighs from the tree-tops, and the languid stretching of wakened and unclasping boughs. Madison Wayne had not, alas! taken into account this subtle conspiracy of Night and Nature, and as he climbed higher, his steps began to falter with new and strange sensations. The rigidity of purpose which had guided the hard religious convictions that always sustained him, began to relax. A tender sympathy stole over him; a loving mercy to himself as well as others stole into his heart. He thought of HER as she had nestled at his side, hand in hand, upon the moonlit veranda of her father's house, before his hard convictions had chilled and affrighted her. He thought of her fresh simplicity, and what had seemed to him her wonderful girlish beauty, and lo! in a quick turn of the path he stood breathless and tremulous before the house. The moonbeams lay tenderly upon the peaceful eaves; the long blossoms of the Madeira vine seemed sleeping also. The pink flush of the Cherokee rose in the unreal light had become chastely white.

But he was evidently too late for an interview. The windows were blank in the white light; only one—her bedroom—showed a light behind the lowered muslin blind. Her draped shadow once or twice passed across it. He was turning away with soft steps and even bated breath when suddenly he stopped. The exaggerated but unmistakable shadow of a man stood beside her on the blind.

With a fierce leap as of a maniac, he was at the door, pounding, rattling, and uttering hoarse and furious outcries. Even through his fury he heard quickened foot-steps—her light, reckless, half-hysterical laugh—a bound upon the staircase—the hurried unbolting and opening of distant doors, as the lighter one with which he was struggling at last yielded to his blind rage, and threw him crashing into the sitting-room. The back door was wide open. He could hear the rustling and crackling of twigs and branches in different directions down the hillside, where the fugitives had separated as they escaped. And yet he stood there for an instant, dazed and wondering, "What next?"

His eyes fell upon McGee's rifle standing upright in the corner. It was a clean, beautiful, precise weapon, even to the unprofessional eye, its long, laminated hexagonal barrel taking a tenderer blue in the moonlight. He snatched it up. It was capped and loaded. Without a pause he dashed down the hill.

Only one thought was in his mind now—the crudest, simplest duty. He was there in McGee's place; he should do what McGee would do. God had abandoned him, but McGee's rifle remained.

In a few minutes' downward plunging he had reached the river bank. The tranquil silver surface quivered and glittered before him. He saw what he knew he would see, the black target of a man's head above it, making for the

Bar. He took deliberate aim and fired. There was no echo to that sharp detonation; a distant dog barked, there was a slight whisper in the trees beside him, that was all! But the head of the man was no longer visible, and the liquid silver filmed over again, without a speck or stain.

He shouldered the rifle, and with the automatic action of men in great crises returned slowly and deliberately to the house and carefully replaced the rifle in its old position. He had no concern for the miserable woman who had fled; had she appeared before him at the moment, he would not have noticed her. Yet a strange instinct—it seemed to him the vaguest curiosity—made him ascend the stairs and enter her chamber. The candle was still burning on the table with that awful unconsciousness and simplicity of detail which makes the scene of real tragedy so terrible. Beside it lay a belt and leather pouch. Madison Wayne suddenly dashed forward and seized it, with a wild, inarticulate cry; staggered, fell over the chair, rose to his feet, blindly groped his way down the staircase, burst into the road, and, hugging the pouch to his bosom, fled like a madman down the hill.

*****

The body of Arthur Wayne was picked up two days later a dozen miles down the river. Nothing could be more evident and prosaic than the manner in which he had met his fate. His body was only partly clothed, and the money pouch and belt, which had been securely locked next his skin, after the fashion of all miners, was gone. He was known to have left the Bar with a considerable sum of money; he was undoubtedly dogged, robbed, and murdered during his journey on the river bank by the desperadoes who were beginning to infest the vicinity. The grief and agony of his only brother, sole survivor of that fraternal and religious partnership so well known to the camp, although shown only by a grim and speechless melancholy,—broken by unintelligible outbursts of religious raving,—was so real, that it affected even the callous camp. But scarcely had it regained its feverish distraction, before it was thrilled by another sensation. Alexander McGee had fallen from the deck of a Sacramento steamboat in the Straits of Carquinez, and his body had been swept out to sea. The news had apparently been first to reach the ears of his devoted wife, for when the camp —at this lapse of the old prohibition—climbed to her bower with their rude consolations, the house was found locked and deserted. The fateful influence of the promontory had again prevailed, the grim record of its seclusion was once more unbroken.

For with it, too, drooped and faded the fortunes of the Bar. Madison Wayne sold out his claim, endowed the church at the Cross Roads with the proceeds, and the pulpit with his grim, hopeless, denunciatory presence. The first rains brought a freshet to the Bar. The river leaped the light barriers that had taken the place of Wayne's peaceful engines, and regained the old channel. The curse that the Rev. Madison Wayne had launched on this riverside Sodom seemed to have been fulfilled. But even this brought no satisfaction to the gloomy prophet, for it was presently known that he had abandoned his terror-stricken flock to take the circuit as revivalist preacher and camp-meeting exhorter, in the rudest and most lawless of gatherings. Desperate ruffians writhed at his feet in impotent terror or more impotent rage; murderers and thieves listened to him with blanched faces and set teeth, restrained only by a more awful fear. Over and over again he took his life with his Bible into his own hands when he rose above the excited multitude; he was shot at, he was rail-ridden, he was deported, but never silenced. And so, sweeping over the country, carrying fear and frenzy with him, scouting life and mercy, and crushing alike the guilty and innocent, he came one Sabbath to a rocky crest of the Sierras—the last tattered and frayed and soiled fringe of civilization on the opened tract of a great highway. And here he was to "testify," as was his wont.

But not as he expected. For as he stood up on a boulder above the thirty or forty men sitting or lying upon other rocks and boulders around him, on the craggy mountain shelf where they had gathered, a man also rose, elbowed past them, and with a hurried impulse tried to descend the declivity. But a cry was suddenly heard from others, quick and clamoring, which called the whole assembly to its feet, and it was seen that the fugitive had in some blundering way fallen from the precipice.

He was brought up cruelly maimed and mangled, his ribs crushed, and one lung perforated, but still breathing and conscious. He had asked to see the preacher. Death impending, and even then struggling with his breath, made this request imperative. Madison Wayne stopped the service, and stalked grimly and inflexibly to where the dying man lay. But there he started.

"McGee!" he said breathlessly.

"Send these men away," said McGee faintly. "I've got suthin' to tell you."

The men drew back without a word. "You thought I was dead," said McGee, with eyes still undimmed and marvelously clear. "I orter bin, but it don't need no doctor to say it ain't far off now. I left the Bar to get killed; I tried to in a row, but the fellows were skeert to close with me, thinkin' I'd shoot. My reputation was agin me, there! You follow me? You understand what I mean?"

Kneeling beside him now and grasping both his hands, the changed and horror-stricken Wayne gasped, "But"—

"Hold on! I jumped off the Sacramento boat—I was goin' down the third time—they thought on the boat I was gone—they think so now! But a passin' fisherman dived for me. I grappled him—he was clear grit and would have gone down with me, but I couldn't let him die too—havin' so to speak no cause. You follow me—you understand me? I let him save me. But it was all the same, for when I got to 'Frisco I read as how I was drowned. And then I reckoned it was all right, and I wandered HERE, where I wasn't known—until I saw you."

"But why should you want to die?" said Wayne, almost fiercely. "What right have you to die while others—double-dyed and blood-stained, are condemned to live, 'testify,' and suffer?"

The dying man feebly waved a deprecation with his maimed hand, and even smiled faintly. "I knew you'd say that. I knew what you'd think about it, but it's all the same now. I did it for you and Safie! I knew I was in the way; I knew you was the man she orter had; I knew you was the man who had dragged her outer the mire and clay where I was leavin' her, as you did when she fell in the water. I knew that every day I lived I was makin' YOU suffer and breakin' HER heart—for all she tried to be gentle and gay."

"Great God in heaven! Will you stop!" said Wayne, springing to his feet in agony. A frightened look—the first that any one had ever seen in the clear eyes of the

Bell-ringer of Angel's—passed over them, and he murmured tremulously: "All right—I'm stoppin'!"

So, too, was his heart, for the wonderful eyes were now slowly glazing. Yet he rallied once more—coming up again the third time as it seemed to Wayne—and his lips moved slowly. The preacher threw himself despairingly on the ground beside him.

"Speak, brother! For God's sake, speak!"

It was his last whisper—so faint it might have been the first of his freed soul. But he only said:—

"You're—followin'—me? You—understand—what—I—mean?"

JOHNNYBOY

The vast dining-room of the Crustacean Hotel at Greyport, U. S., was empty and desolate. It was so early in the morning that there was a bedroom deshabille in the tucked-up skirts and bare legs of the little oval breakfast-tables as they had just been left by the dusting servants. The most stirring of travelers was yet abed, the most enterprising of first-train catchers had not yet come down; there was a breath of midsummer sleep still in the air; through the half-opened windows that seemed to be yawning, the pinkish blue Atlantic beyond heaved gently and slumberously, and drowsy early bathers crept into it as to bed. Yet as I entered the room I saw that one of the little tables in the corner was in reality occupied by a very small and very extraordinary child. Seated in a high chair, attended by a dreamily abstracted nurse on one side, an utterly perfunctory negro waiter on the other, and an incongruous assortment of disregarded viands before him, he was taking—or, rather, declining—his solitary break-fast. He appeared to be a pale, frail, but rather pretty boy, with a singularly pathetic combination of infant delicacy of outline and maturity of expression. His heavily fringed eyes expressed an already weary and discontented intelligence, and his willful, resolute little mouth was, I fancied, marked with lines of pain at either corner. He struck me as not only being physically dyspeptic, but as

Bret Harte

morally loathing his attendants and surroundings.

My entrance did not disturb the waiter, with whom I had no financial relations; he simply concealed an exaggerated yawn professionally behind his napkin until my own servitor should appear. The nurse slightly awoke from her abstraction, shoved the child mechanically,—as if starting up some clogged machinery,—said, "Eat your breakfast, Johnnyboy," and subsided into her dream. I think the child had at first some faint hope of me, and when my waiter appeared with my breakfast he betrayed some interest in my selection, with a view of possible later appropriation, but, as my repast was simple, that hope died out of his infant mind. Then there was a silence, broken at last by the languid voice of the nurse:—

"Try some milk then—nice milk."

"No! No mik! Mik makes me sick—mik does!"

In spite of the hurried infantine accent the protest was so emphatic, and, above all, fraught with such pent-up reproach and disgust, that I turned about sympathetically. But Johnnyboy had already thrown down his spoon, slipped from his high chair, and was marching out of the room as fast as his little sandals would carry him, with indignation bristling in every line of the crisp bows of his sash.

I, however, gathered from Mr. Johnson, my waiter, that the unfortunate child owned a fashionable father and mother, one or two blocks of houses in New York, and a villa at Greyport, which he consistently and intelligently despised. That he had imperiously brought his parents here on account of his health, and had demanded that he should breakfast alone in the big dining-room. That, however, he was not happy. "Nuffin peahs to agree wid him, Sah, but he doan' cry, and he speaks his mind, Sah; he speaks his mind."

Unfortunately, I did not keep Johnnyboy's secret, but related the scene I had witnessed to some of the lighter-hearted Crustaceans of either sex, with the result that his alliterative protest became a sort of catchword among them, and that for the next few mornings he had a large audience of early breakfasters, who fondly hoped for a repetition of his performance. I think that Johnnyboy for the time enjoyed this companionship, yet without the least affection or self-consciousness—so long as it was unobtrusive. It so chanced, however, that the Rev. Mr. Belcher, a gentleman with bovine lightness of touch, and a singular misunderstanding of childhood, chose to presume upon his paternal functions. Approaching the high chair in which Johnnyboy was dyspeptically reflecting, with a ponderous wink at the other guests, and a fat thumb and forefinger on Johnnyboy's table, he leaned over him, and with slow, elephantine playfulness said:—

"And so, my dear young friend, I understand that 'mik makes you sick—mik does.'"

Anything approaching to the absolute likeness of this imitation of Johnnyboy's accents it is impossible to conceive. Possibly Johnnyboy felt it. But he simply lifted his lovely lashes, and said with great distinctness:—

"Mik don't—you devil!"

After this, closely as it had knitted us together, Johnnyboy's morning presence was mysteriously withdrawn. It was later pointed out to us by Mr. Belcher, upon the veranda, that, although Wealth had its privileges, it was held in trust for the welfare of Mankind, and that the children of the Rich could not too early learn the advantages of Self-restraint and the vanity of a mere gratification of the Senses. Early and frequent morning ablutions, brisk morning toweling, half of a Graham biscuit in a teacup of milk, exercise with the dumb-bells, and a little rough-and-tumble play in a straw hat, check apron, and overalls would eventually improve that stamina necessary for his future Position, and repress a dangerous cerebral activity and tendency to give way to— He suddenly stopped, coughed, and absolutely looked embarrassed. Johnnyboy, a moving cloud of white pique, silk, and embroidery, had just turned the corner of the veranda. He did not speak, but as he passed raised his blue-veined lids to the orator. The look of ineffable scorn and superiority in those beautiful eyes surpassed anything I had ever seen. At the next veranda column he paused, and, with his baby thumbs inserted in his silk sash, again regarded him under his half-dropped lashes as if he were some curious animal, and then passed on. But Belcher was silenced for the second time.

I think I have said enough to show that Johnnyboy was hopelessly worshiped by an impressible and illogical sex. I say HOPELESSLY, for he slipped equally from the proudest silken lap and the humblest one of calico, and carried his eyelashes and small aches elsewhere. I think that a secret fear of his alarming frankness, and his steady rejection of the various tempting cates they offered him, had much to do with their passion. "It won't hurt you, dear," said Miss Circe, "and it's so awfully nice. See!" she continued, putting one of the delicacies in her own pretty mouth with every assumption of delight. "It's SO good!" Johnnyboy rested his elbows on her knees, and watched her with a grieved and commiserating superiority.

"Bimeby, you'll have pains in youse tommick, and you'll be tookt to bed," he said sadly, "and then you'll—have to dit up and"—But as it was found necessary here to repress further details, he escaped other temptation.

Two hours later, as Miss Circe was seated in the drawing-room with her usual circle of enthusiastic admirers around her, Johnnyboy—who was issued from his room for circulation, two or three times a day, as a genteel advertisement of his parents—floated into the apartment in a new dress and a serious demeanor. Sidling up to Miss Circe he laid a phial—evidently his own pet medicine—on her lap, said, "For youse tommikake to-night," and vanished. Yet I have reason to believe that this slight evidence of unusual remembrance on Johnnyboy's part more than compensated for its publicity, and for a few days Miss Circe was quite "set up" by it.

It was through some sympathy of this kind that I first gained Johnnyboy's good graces. I had been presented with a small pocket case of homoeopathic medicines, and one day on the beach I took out one of the tiny phials and, dropping two or three of the still tinier pellets in my hand, swallowed them. To my embarrassment, a small hand presently grasped my trouser-leg. I looked down; it was Johnnyboy, in a new and ravishing smuggler suit, with his questioning eyes fixed on mine.

"Howjer do dat?"

"Eh?"

"Wajer do dat for?"

"That?—Oh, that's medicine. I've got a headache."

Bret Harte

He searched the inmost depths of my soul with his wonderful eyes. Then, after a pause, he held out his baby palm.

"You kin give Johnny some."

"But you haven't got headache—have you?"

"Me alluz has."

"Not ALWAYS."

He nodded his head rapidly. Then added slowly, and with great elaboration, "Et mo'nins, et affernoons, et nights, 'nd mo'nins adain. 'N et becker" (i. e., breakfast).

There was no doubt it was the truth. Those eyes did not seem to be in the habit of lying. After all, the medicine could not hurt him. His nurse was at a little distance gazing absently at the sea. I sat down on a bench, and dropped a few of the pellets into his palm. He ate them seriously, and then turned around and backed—after the well-known appealing fashion of childhood—against my knees. I understood the movement—although it was unlike my idea of Johnnyboy. However, I raised him to my lap—with the sensation of lifting a dozen lace-edged handkerchiefs, and with very little more effort—where he sat silently for a moment, with his sandals crossed pensively before him.

"Wouldn't you like to go and play with those children?" I asked, pointing to a group of noisy sand levelers not far away.

"No!" After a pause, "You wouldn't neither."

"Why?"

"Hediks."

"But," I said, "perhaps if you went and played with them and ran up and down as they do, you wouldn't have headache."

Johnnyboy did not answer for a moment; then there was a perceptible gentle movement of his small frame. I confess I felt brutally like Belcher. He was getting down.

Once down he faced me, lifted his frank eyes, said, "Do way and play den," smoothed down his smuggler frock, and rejoined his nurse.

But although Johnnyboy afterwards forgave my moral defection, he did not seem to have forgotten my practical medical ministration, and our brief interview had a surprising result. From that moment he confounded his parents and doctors by resolutely and positively refusing to take any more of their pills, tonics, or drops. Whether from a sense of loyalty to me, or whether he was not yet convinced of the efficacy of homoeopathy, he did not suggest a substitute, declare his preferences, or even give his reasons, but firmly and peremptorily declined his present treatment. And, to everybody's astonishment, he did not seem a bit the worse for it.

Still he was not strong, and his continual aversion to childish sports and youthful exercise provoked the easy criticism of that large part of humanity who are ready to confound cause and effect, and such brief moments as the Sluysdaels could spare him from their fashionable duties were made miserable to them by gratuitous suggestions and plans for their child's improvement. It was noticeable, however, that few of them were ever offered to Johnnyboy personally. He had a singularly direct way of dealing with them, and a precision of statement that was embarrassing.

One afternoon, Jack Bracy drove up to the veranda of the Crustacean with a smart buggy and spirited thoroughbred for Miss Circe's especial driving, and his own saddle-horse on which he was to accompany her. Jack had dismounted, a groom held his saddle-horse until the young lady should appear, and he himself stood at the head of the thoroughbred. As Johnnyboy, leaning against the railing, was regarding the turnout with ill-concealed disdain, Jack, in the pride of his triumph over his rivals, good-humoredly offered to put him in the buggy, and allow him to take the reins. Johnnyboy did not reply.

"Come along!" continued Jack, "it will do you a heap of good! It's better than lazing there like a girl! Rouse up, old man!"

"Me don't like that geegee," said Johnnyboy calmly. "He's a silly fool."

"You're afraid," said Jack.

Johnnyboy lifted his proud lashes, and toddled to the steps. Jack received him in his arms, swung him into the seat, and placed the slim yellow reins in his baby hands.

"Now you feel like a man, and not like a girl!" said Jack. "Eh, what? Oh, I beg your pardon."

For Miss Circe had appeared—had absolutely been obliged to wait a whole half-minute unobserved—and now stood there a dazzling but pouting apparition. In eagerly turning to receive her, Jack's foot slipped on the step, and he fell. The thoroughbred started, gave a sickening plunge forward, and was off! But so, too, was Jack, the next moment, on his own horse, and before Miss Circe's screams had died away.

For two blocks on Ocean Avenue, passersby that afternoon saw a strange vision. A galloping horse careering before a light buggy, in which a small child, seated upright, was grasping the tightened reins. But so erect and composed was the little face and figure—albeit as white as its own frock—that for an instant they did not grasp its awful significance. Those further along, however, read the whole awful story in the drawn face and blazing eyes of Jack Bracy as he, at last, swung into the Avenue. For Jack had the brains as well as the nerve of your true hero, and, knowing the dangerous stimulus of a stern chase to a frightened horse, had kept a side road until it branched into the Avenue. So furious had been his pace, and so correct his calculation, that he ranged alongside of the runaway even as it passed, grasped the reins, and, in half a block, pulled up on even wheels.

"I never saw such pluck in a mite like that," he whispered afterwards to his anxious auditory. "He never dropped those ribbons, by G——, until I got alongside, and then he just hopped down and said, as short and cool as you please, 'Dank you!'"

"Me didn't," uttered a small voice reproachfully.

"Didn't you, dear! What DID you say then, darling?" exclaimed a sympathizing chorus.

"Me said: 'Damn you!' Me don't like silly fool geegees. Silly fool geegees make me sick—silly fool geegees do!"

Nevertheless, in spite of this incident, the attempts at Johnnyboy's physical reformation still went on. More than that, it was argued by some complacent casuists that the pluck displayed by the child was the actual result of this somewhat heroic method of taking exercise, and NOT an inherent manliness distinct from his physical tastes. So he was made to run when he didn't want to—to dance when he frankly loathed his partners—to play at games that he despised. His books and pictures were taken away; he was hurried past hoardings and theatrical posters that engaged his fancy; the public was warned against telling him fairy tales, except those constructed on strictly hygienic principles. His fastidious cleanliness was rebuked, and his best frocks taken away—albeit at a terrible sacrifice of his parents' vanity—to suit the theories of his critics. How long this might have continued is not known—for the theory and practice were suddenly arrested by another sensation.

One morning a children's picnic party was given on a rocky point only accessible at certain states of the tide, whither they were taken in a small boat under the charge of a few hotel servants, and, possibly as part of his heroic treatment, Johnnyboy, who was included in the party, was not allowed to be attended by his regular nurse.

Whether this circumstance added to his general disgust of the whole affair, and his unwillingness to go, I cannot say, but it is to be regretted, since the omission deprived Johnnyboy of any impartial witness to what subsequently occurred. That he was somewhat roughly handled by several of the larger children appeared to be beyond doubt, although there was conflicting evidence as to the sequel. Enough that at noon screams were heard in the direction of certain detached rocks on the point, and the whole party proceeding thither found three of the larger boys on the rocks, alone and cut off by the tide, having been left there, as they alleged, by Johnnyboy, WHO HAD RUN AWAY WITH THE BOAT. They subsequently admitted that THEY had first taken the boat and brought Johnnyboy with them, "just to frighten him," but they adhered to the rest. And certainly Johnnyboy and the boat were nowhere to be found. The shore was communicated with, the alarm was given, the telegraph, up and down the coast trilled with excitement, other boats were manned—consternation prevailed.

But that afternoon the captain of the "Saucy Jane," mackerel fisher, lying off the point, perceived a derelict "Whitehall" boat drifting lazily towards the Gulf Stream. On boarding it he was chagrined to find the expected flotsam already in the possession of a very small child, who received him with a scornful reticence as regarded himself and his intentions, and some objurgation of a person or persons unknown. It was Johnnyboy. But whether he had attempted the destruction of the three other boys by "marooning" them upon the rocks—as their parents firmly believed—or whether he had himself withdrawn from their company simply because he did not like them, was never known. Any further attempt to improve his education by the roughing gregarious process was, however, abandoned. The very critics who had counseled it now clamored for restraint and perfect isolation. It was ably pointed out by the Rev. Mr. Belcher that the autocratic habits begotten by wealth and pampering should be restricted, and all intercourse with their possessor promptly withheld.

But the season presently passed with much of this and other criticism, and the Sluysdaels passed too, carrying Johnnyboy and his small aches and long eyelashes beyond these Crustacean voices, where it was to be hoped there was peace. I did not hear of him again for five years, and then, oddly enough, from the lips of Mr. Belcher on the deck of a transatlantic steamer, as he was being wafted to Europe for his recreation by the prayers and purses of a grateful and enduring flock. "Master John Jacob Astor Sluysdael," said Mr. Belcher, speaking slowly, with great precision of retrospect, "was taken from his private governess—I may say by my advice—and sent to an admirable school in New York, fashioned upon the English system of Eton and Harrow, and conducted by English masters from Oxford and Cambridge. Here—I may also say at my suggestion—he was subjected to the wholesome discipline equally of his schoolmates and his masters; in fact, sir, as you are probably aware, the most perfect democracy that we have yet known, in which the mere accidents of wealth, position, luxury, effeminacy, physical degeneration, and over-civilized stimulation, are not recognized. He was put into compulsory cricket, football, and rounders. As an undersized boy he was subjected to that ingenious preparation for future mastership by the pupillary state of servitude known, I think, as 'fagging.' His physical inertia was stimulated and quickened, and his intellectual precocity repressed, from time to time, by the exuberant playfulness of his fellow-students, which occasionally took the form of forced ablutions and corporal discomfort, and was called, I am told, 'hazing.' It is but fair to state that our young friend had some singular mental endowments, which, however, were promptly checked to repress the vanity and presumption that would follow." The Rev. Mr. Belcher paused, closed his eyes resignedly, and added, "Of course, you know the rest."

"Indeed, I do not," I said anxiously.

"A most deplorable affair—indeed, a most shocking

incident! It was hushed up, I believe, on account of the position of his parents." He glanced furtively around, and in a lower and more impressive voice said, "I am not myself a believer in heredity, and I am not personally aware that there was a MURDERER among the Sluysdael ancestry, but it seems that this monstrous child, in some clandestine way, possessed himself of a huge bowie-knife, sir, and on one of those occasions actually rushed furiously at the larger boys—his innocent play-fellows—and absolutely forced them to flee in fear of their lives. More than that, sir, a LOADED REVOLVER was found in his desk, and he boldly and shamelessly avowed his intention to eviscerate, or—to use his own revolting language—'to cut the heart out' of the first one who again 'laid a finger on him.'" He paused again, and, joining his two hands together with the fingers pointing to the deck, breathed hard and said, "His instantaneous withdrawal from the school was a matter of public necessity. He was afterwards taken, in the charge of a private tutor, to Europe, where, I trust, we shall NOT meet."

I could not resist saying cheerfully that, at least, Johnnyboy had for a short time made it lively for the big boys.

The Rev. Mr. Belcher rose slowly, but painfully, said with a deeply grieved expression, "I don't think that I entirely follow you," and moved gently away.

The changes of youth are apt to be more bewildering than those of age, and a decade scarcely perceptible in an old civilization often means utter revolution to the new. It did not seem strange to me, therefore, on meeting Jack Bracy twelve years after, to find that he had forgotten Miss Circe, or that SHE had married, and was living unhappily with a middle-aged adventurer by the name of Jason, who was reputed to have had domestic relations elsewhere. But although subjugated and exorcised, she at least was reminiscent. To my inquiries about the Sluysdaels, she answered with a slight return of her old vivacity:—

"Ah, yes, dear fellow, he was one of my greatest admirers."

"He was about four years old when you knew him, wasn't he?" suggested Jason meanly. "Yes, they usually WERE young, but so kind of you to recollect them. Young Sluysdael," he continued, turning to me, "is—but of course you know that disgraceful story."

I felt that I could stand this no longer. "Yes," I said indignantly, "I know all about the school, and I don't call his conduct disgraceful either."

Jason stared. "I don't know what you mean about the school," he returned. "I am speaking of his stepfather."

"His STEPFATHER!"

"Yes; his father, Van Buren Sluysdael, died, you know—a year after they left Greyport. The widow was left all the money in trust for Johnny, except about twenty-five hundred a year which he was in receipt of as a separate income, even as a boy. Well, a glib-tongued parson, a fellow by the name of Belcher, got round the widow—she was a desperate fool—and, by Jove! made her marry him. He made ducks and drakes of not only her money, but Johnny's too, and had to skip to Spain to avoid the trustees. And Johnny—for the Sluysdaels are all fools or lunatics—made over his whole separate income to that wretched, fashionable fool of a mother, and went into a stockbroker's office as a clerk."

"And walks to business before eight every morning, and they say even takes down the shutters and sweeps out," broke in Circe impulsively. "Works like a slave all day, wears out his old clothes, has given up his clubs and amusements, and shuns society."

"But how about his health?" I asked. "Is he better and stronger?"

"I don't know," said Circe, "but he LOOKS as beautiful as Endymion."

*****

At his bank, in Wall Street, Bracy that afternoon confirmed all that Jason had told me of young Sluysdael. "But his temper?" I asked. "You remember his temper—surely."

"He's as sweet as a lamb, never quarrels, never whines, never alludes to his lost fortune, and is never put out. For a youngster, he's the most popular man in the street. Shall we nip round and see him?"

"By all means."

"Come. It isn't far."

A few steps down the crowded street we dived into a den of plate-glass windows, of scraps of paper, of rattling, ticking machines, more voluble and excited than the careworn, abstracted men who leaned over them. But "Johnnyboy"—I started at the familiar name again—was not there. He was at luncheon.

"Let us join him," I said, as we gained the street again and turned mechanically into Delmonico's.

"Not there," said Bracy with a laugh. "You forget! That's not Johnnyboy's gait just now. Come here." He was descending a few steps that led to a humble cake-shop. As we entered I noticed a young fellow standing before the plain wooden counter with a cake of gingerbread in one hand and a glass of milk in the other. His profile was before me; I at once recognized the long lashes. But the happy, boyish, careless laugh that greeted Bracy, as he presented me, was a revelation.

Yet he was pleased to remember me. And then—it may have been embarrassment that led me to such tactlessness, but as I glanced at him and the glass of milk he was holding, I could not help reminding him of the first words I had ever heard him utter.

He tossed off the glass, colored slightly, as I thought, and said with a light laugh:—

"I suppose I have changed a good deal since then, sir."

I looked at his demure and resolute mouth, and wondered if he had.

YOUNG ROBIN GRAY

The good American barque Skyscraper was swinging at
her moorings in the Clyde, off Bannock, ready for sea.
But that good American barque—although owned in
Baltimore—had not a plank of American timber in her
hulk, nor a native American in her crew, and even her
nautical "goodness" had been called into serious question
by divers of that crew during her voyage, and answered
more or less inconclusively with belaying-pins, marlin-
spikes, and ropes' ends at the hands of an Irish-American
captain and a Dutch and Danish mate. So much so, that
the mysterious powers of the American consul at St.
Kentigern had been evoked to punish mutiny on the one
hand, and battery and starvation on the other; both equally
attested by manifestly false witness and subornation on
each side. In the exercise of his functions the consul had
opened and shut some jail doors, and otherwise effected
the usual sullen and deceitful compromise, and his flag
was now flying, on a final visit, from the stern sheets of a
smart boat alongside. It was with a feeling of relief at the
end of the interview that he at last lifted his head above an
atmosphere of perjury and bilge-water and came on deck.
The sun and wind were ruffling and glinting on the
broadening river beyond the "measured mile"; a few gulls
were wavering and dipping near the lee scuppers, and the
sound of Sabbath bells, mellowed by a distance that

Bret Harte

secured immunity of conscience, came peacefully to his ear.

"Now that job's over ye'll be takin' a partin' dhrink," suggested the captain.

The consul thought not. Certain incidents of "the job" were fresh in his memory, and he proposed to limit himself to his strict duty.

"You have some passengers, I see," he said, pointing to a group of two men and a young girl, who had apparently just come aboard.

"Only wan; an engineer going out to Rio. Them's just his friends seein' him off, I'm thinkin'," returned the captain, surveying them somewhat contemptuously.

The consul was a little disturbed. He wondered if the passenger knew anything of the quality and reputation of the ship to which he was entrusting his fortunes. But he was only a PASSENGER, and the consul's functions—like those of the aloft-sitting cherub of nautical song—were restricted exclusively to looking after "Poor Jack." However, he asked a few further questions, eliciting the fact that the stranger had already visited the ship with letters from the eminently respectable consignees at St. Kentigern, and contented himself with lingering near them. The young girl was accompanied by her father, a respectably rigid-looking middle-class tradesman, who, however, seemed to be more interested in the novelty of his surroundings than in the movements of his daughter and their departing friend. So it chanced that the consul re-entered the cabin—ostensibly in search of a missing glove, but really with the intention of seeing how the passenger was bestowed—just behind them. But to his great embarrassment he at once perceived that, owing to the obscurity of the apartment, they had not noticed him, and before he could withdraw, the man had passed his arm around the young girl's half stiffened, yet half yielding figure.

"Only one, Ailsa," he pleaded in a slow, serious voice, pathetic from the very absence of any youthful passion in it; "just one now. It'll be gey lang before we meet again. Ye'll not refuse me now."

The young girl's lips seemed to murmur some protest that, however, was lost in the beginning of a long and silent kiss.

The consul slipped out softly. His smile had died away. That unlooked-for touch of human weakness seemed to purify the stuffy and evil-reeking cabin, and the recollection of its brutal past to drop with a deck-load of iniquity behind him to the bottom of the Clyde. It is to be feared that in his unofficial moments he was inclined to be sentimental, and it seemed to him that the good ship Skyscraper henceforward carried an innocent freight not mentioned in her manifest, and that a gentle, ever-smiling figure, not entered on her books, had invisibly taken a place at her wheel.

But he was recalled to himself by a slight altercation on deck. The young girl and the passenger had just returned from the cabin. The consul, after a discreetly careless pause, had lifted his eyes to the young girl's face, and saw that it was singularly pretty in color and outline, but perfectly self-composed and serenely unconscious. And he was a little troubled to observe that the passenger was a middle-aged man, whose hard features were already considerably worn with trial and experience.

Both he and the girl were listening with sympathizing but cautious interest to her father's contention with the boatman who had brought them from shore, and who was now inclined to demand an extra fee for returning with them. The boatman alleged that he had been detained beyond "kirk time," and that this imperiling of his salva-tion could only be compensated by another shilling. To the consul's surprise, this extraordinary argument was recognized by the father, who, however, contented himself by simply contending that it had not been stipulated in the bargain. The issue was, therefore, limited, and the discussion progressed slowly and deliberately, with a certain calm dignity and argumen-tative satisfaction on both sides that exalted the subject, though it irritated the captain.

"If ye accept the premisses that I've just laid down, that it's a contract"—began the boatman.

"Dry up! and haul off," said the captain.

"One moment," interposed the consul, with a rapid glance at the slight trouble in the young girl's face. Turning to the father, he went on: "Will you allow me to offer you and your daughter a seat in my boat?"

It was an unlooked-for and tempting proposal. The boatman was lazily lying on his oars, secure in self-righteousness and the conscious possession of the only available boat to shore; on the other hand, the smart gig of the consul, with its four oars, was not only a providential escape from a difficulty, but even to some extent a quasi-official endorsement of his contention. Yet he hesitated.

"It'll be costin' ye no more?" he said interrogatively, glancing at the consul's boat crew, "or ye'll be askin' me a fair proportion."

"It will be the gentleman's own boat," said the girl, with a certain shy assurance, "and he'll be paying his boatmen by the day."

The consul hastened to explain that their passage would involve no additional expense to anybody, and added, tactfully, that he was glad to enable them to oppose extortion.

"Ay, but it's a preencipel," said the father proudly, "and I'm pleased, sir, to see ye recognize it."

He proceeded to help his daughter into the boat without any further leave-taking of the passenger, to the consul's great surprise, and with only a parting nod from the young girl. It was as if this momentous incident were a sufficient reason for the absence of any further trivial sentiment.

Unfortunately the father chose to add an exordium for the benefit of the astonished boatsman still lying on his oars.

"Let this be a lesson to ye, ma frien', when ye're ower sure! Ye'll ne'er say a herrin' is dry until it be reestit an' reekit."

"Ay," said the boatman, with a lazy, significant glance at the consul, "it wull be a lesson to me not to trust to a lassie's GANGIN' jo, when thair's anither yin comin'."

"Give way," said the consul sharply.

Yet his was the only irritated face in the boat as the men bent over their oars. The young girl and her father looked placidly at the receding ship, and waved their hands to the grave, resigned face over the taffrail. The consul examined them more attentively. The father's face showed intelligence and a certain probity in its otherwise commonplace features. The young girl had more distinction, with, perhaps, more delicacy of outline than of texture. Her hair was dark, with a burnished copper tint at its roots, and eyes that had the same burnished metallic lustre in their brown pupils. Both sat respectfully erect, as if anxious to record the fact that the boat was not their own to take their ease in; and both were silently reserved, answering briefly to the consul's remarks as if to indicate the formality of their presence there. But a distant railway whistle startled them into emotion.

"We've lost the train, father!" said the young girl.

The consul followed the direction of her anxious eyes; the train was just quitting the station at Bannock.

"If ye had not lingered below with Jamie, we'd have been away in time, ay, and in our own boat," said the father, with marked severity.

The consul glanced quickly at the girl. But her face betrayed no consciousness, except of their present disappointment.

"There's an excursion boat coming round the Point," he said, pointing to the black smoke trail of a steamer at the entrance of a loch, "and it will be returning to St. Kentigern shortly. If you like, we'll pull over and put you aboard."

"Eh! but it's the Sabbath-breaker!" said the old man harshly.

The consul suddenly remembered that that was the name which the righteous St. Kentigerners had given to the solitary bold, bad pleasure-boat that defied their Sabbatical observances.

"Perhaps you won't find very pleasant company on board," said the consul smiling; "but, then, you're not seeking THAT. And as you would be only using the boat to get back to your home, and not for Sunday recreation, I don't think your conscience should trouble you."

"Ay, that's a fine argument, Mr. Consul, but I'm thinkin' it's none the less sopheestry for a' that," said the father grimly. "No; if ye'll just land us yonder at Bannock pier, we'll be ay thankin' ye the same."

"But what will you do there? There's no other train to-day."

"Ay, we'll walk on a bit."

The consul was silent. After a pause the young girl lifted her clear eyes, and with a half pathetic, half childish politeness, said: "We'll be doing very well—my father and me. You're far too kind."

Nothing further was said as they began to thread their way between a few large ships and an ocean steamer at anchor, from whose decks a few Sunday-clothed mariners gazed down admiringly on the smart gig and the pretty girl in a Tam o' Shanter in its stern sheets. But here a new idea struck the consul. A cable's length ahead lay a yacht, owned by an American friend, and at her stern a steam launch swung to its painter. Without intimating his intention to his passengers he steered for it. "Bow!—way enough," he called out as the boat glided under the yacht's counter, and, grasping the companion-ladder ropes, he leaped aboard. In a few hurried words he explained the situation to Mr. Robert Gray, her owner, and suggested that he should send the belated passengers to St. Kentigern by the launch. Gray assented with the easy good-nature of youth, wealth, and indolence, and lounged from his cabin to the side. The consul followed. Looking down upon the boat he could not help observing that his fair young passenger, sitting in her demure stillness at her father's side, made a very pretty picture. It was possible that "Bob Gray" had made the same observation, for he presently swung himself over the gangway into the gig, hat in hand. The launch could easily take them; in fact, he added unblushingly, it was even then getting up steam to go to St. Kentigern. Would they kindly come on board until it was ready? At an added word or two of explanation from the consul, the father accepted, preserving the same formal pride and stiffness, and the transfer was made. The consul, looking back as his gig swept round again towards Bannock pier, received their parting salutations, and the first smile he had seen on the face of his grave little passenger. He thought it very sweet and sad.

He did not return to the Consulate at St. Kentigern until the next day. But he was somewhat surprised to find Mr. Robert Gray awaiting him, and upon some business which the young millionaire could have easily deputed to his captain or steward. As he still lingered, the consul pleasantly referred to his generosity on the previous day, and hoped the passengers had given him no trouble.

"No," said Gray with a slight simulation of carelessness. "In fact I came up with them myself. I had nothing to do; it was Sunday, you know."

The consul lifted his eyebrows slightly.

"Yes, I saw them home," continued Gray lightly. "In one of those by-streets not far from here; neat-looking house outside; inside, corkscrew stone staircase like a lighthouse; fourth floor, no lift, but SHE circled up like a swallow! Flat—sitting-room, two bedrooms, and a kitchen—mighty snug and shipshape and pretty as a pink. They OWN it too—fancy OWNING part of a house! Seems to be a way they have here in St. Kentigern." He paused and then added: "Stayed there to a kind of high tea!"

"Indeed," said the consul.

"Why not? The old man wanted to return my 'hospitality' and square the account! He wasn't going to lie under any obligation to a stranger, and, by Jove! he made it a special point of honor! A Spanish grandee couldn't have been more punctilious. And with an accent, Jerusalem! like a northeaster off the Banks! But the feed was in good taste, and he only a mathematical instrument maker, on about twelve hundred dollars a year!"

"You seem to know all about him," said the consul smilingly.

"Not so much as he does about me," returned Gray, with a half perplexed face; "for he saw enough to admonish me about my extravagance, and even to intimate that that rascal Saunderson, my steward, was imposing on me. SHE took me to task, too, for not laying the yacht up on Sunday that the men could go 'to kirk,' and for swearing at a bargeman who ran across our bows. It's their perfect simplicity and sincerity in all this that gets me! You'd have thought that the old man was my guardian, and the daughter my aunt." After a pause he uttered a reminiscent laugh. "She thought we ate and drank too much on the yacht, and wondered what we could find to do all day. All this, you know, in the gentlest, caressing sort of voice, as if she was really concerned, like one's own sister. Well, not exactly like mine"—he interrupted himself grimly—"but, hang it all, you know what I mean. You know that our girls over there haven't got THAT trick of voice. Too much self-assertion, I reckon; things made too easy for them by us men. Habit of race, I dare say." He laughed a little. "Why, I mislaid my glove when I was coming away, and it was as good as a play to hear her commiserating and sympathizing, and hunting for it as if it were a lost baby."

"But you've seen Scotch girls before this," said the consul. "There were Lady Glairn's daughters, whom you took on a cruise."

"Yes, but the swell Scotch all imitate the English, as everybody else does, for the matter of that, our girls included; and they're all alike. Society makes 'em fit in together like tongued and grooved planks that will take any amount of holy-stoning and polish. It's like dropping into a dead calm, with every rope and spar that you know already reflected back from the smooth water upon you. It's mighty pretty, but it isn't getting on, you know." After a pause he added: "I asked them to take a little holiday cruise with me."

"And they declined," interrupted the consul.

Gray glanced at him quickly.

"Well, yes; that's all right enough. They don't know me, you see, but they do know you; and the fact is, I was thinking that as you're our consul here, don't you see, and sort of responsible for me, you might say that it was all right, you know. Quite the customary thing with us over there. And you might say, generally, who I am."

"I see," said the consul deliberately. "Tell them you're Bob Gray, with more money and time than you know what to do with; that you have a fine taste for yachting and shooting and racing, and amusing yourself generally; that you find that THEY amuse you, and you would like your luxury and your dollars to stand as an equivalent to their independence and originality; that, being a good republican yourself, and recognizing no distinction of class, you don't care what this may mean to them, who are brought up differently; that after their cruise with you you don't care what life, what friends, or what jealousies they return to; that you know no ties, no responsibilities beyond the present, and that you are not a marrying man."

"Look here, I say, aren't you making a little too much of this?" said Gray stiffly.

The consul laughed. "I should be glad to know that I am."

Gray rose. "We'll be dropping down the river to-morrow," he said, with a return of his usual lightness, "and I reckon I'll be toddling down to the wharf. Good-bye, if I don't see you again."

He passed out. As the consul glanced from the window he observed, however, that Mr. Gray was "toddling" in quite another direction than the wharf. For an instant he half regretted that he had not suggested, in some discreet way, the conclusion he had arrived at after witnessing the girl's parting with the middle-aged passenger the day before. But he reflected that this was something he had only accidentally overseen, and was the girl's own secret.

II

When the summer had so waxed in its fullness that the smoke of factory chimneys drifted high, permitting glimpses of fairly blue sky; when the grass in St. Kentigern's proudest park took on a less sober green in the comfortable sun, and even in the thickest shade there was no chilliness, the good St. Kentigerners recognized that the season had arrived to go "down the river," and that it was time for them to betake themselves, with rugs, mackintoshes, and umbrellas, to the breezy lochs and misty hillsides for which the neighborhood of St. Kentigern is justly famous. So when it came to pass that the blinds were down in the highest places, and the most exclusive pavements of St. Kentigern were echoless and desolate, the consul heroically tore himself from the weak delight of basking in the sunshine, and followed the others.

He soon found himself settled at the furthest end of a long narrow loch, made longer and narrower by the steep hillside of rock and heather which flanked its chilly surface on either side, and whose inequalities were lost in the firs and larches that filled ravine and chasm. The fragrant road which ran sinuously through their shadowy depths was invisible from the loch; no protuberance broke the seemingly sheer declivity; the even sky-line was indented in two places—one where it was cracked into a fanciful resemblance to a human profile, the other where it was curved like a bowl. Need it be said that one was distinctly recognized as the silhouette of a prehistoric giant, and that the other was his drinking-cup; need it be added that neither lent the slightest human suggestion to the solitude? A toy-like pier extending into the loch, midway from the barren shore, only heightened the desolation. And when the little steamboat that occasionally entered the loch took away a solitary passenger from the pier-head, the simplest parting was invested with a dreary loneliness that might have brought tears to the most hardened eye.

Still, when the shadow of either hillside was not reaching across the loch, the meridian sun, chancing upon this coy mirror, made the most of it. Then it was that, seen from above, it flashed like a falchion lying between the hills; then its reflected glory, striking up, transfigured the two acclivities, tipped the cold heather with fire, gladdened the funereal pines, and warmed the ascetic rocks. And it was in one of those rare, passionate intervals that the consul, riding along the wooded track and turning his eyes from their splendors, came upon a little house.

It had once been a sturdy cottage, with a grim endurance and inflexibility which even some later and lighter additions had softened rather than changed. On either side of the door, against the bleak whitewashed wall, two tall fuchsias relieved the rigid blankness with a show of color. The windows were prettily draped with curtains caught up with gay ribbons. In a stony pound-like enclosure there was some attempt at floral cultivation, but all quite recent. So, too, were a wicker garden seat, a bright Japanese umbrella, and a tropical hammock suspended between two arctic-looking bushes, which the rude and rigid forefathers of the hamlet would have probably resented.

He had just passed the house when a charming figure slipped across the road before him. To his surprise it was the young girl he had met a few months before on the Skyscraper. But the Tam o' Shanter was replaced by a little straw hat; and a light dress, summery in color and texture, but more in keeping with her rustic surroundings, seemed as grateful and rare as the sunshine. Without knowing why, he had an impression that it was of her own making—a gentle plagiarism of the style of her more fortunate sisters, but with a demure restraint all her own. As she recognized him a faint color came to her cheek, partly from surprise, partly from some association. To his delighted greeting she responded by informing him that her father had taken the cottage he had just passed, where they were spending a three weeks' vacation from his business. It was not so far from St. Kentigern but that he could run up for a day to look after the shop. Did the consul not think it was wise

Quite ready to assent to any sagacity in those clear brown eyes, the consul thought it was. But was it not, like wisdom, sometimes lonely

Ah! no. There was the loch and the hills and the heather; there were her flowers; did he not think they were growing well? and at the head of the loch there was the old tomb of the McHulishes, and some of the coffins were still to be seen.

Perhaps emboldened by the consul's smile, she added, with a more serious precision which was, however, lost in the sympathizing caress of her voice, "And would you not be getting off and coming in and resting a wee bit before you go further? It would be so good of you, and father would think it so kind. And he will be there now, if you're looking."

The consul looked. The old man was standing in the doorway of the cottage, as respectably uncompromising as ever, with the slight concession to his rural surroundings of wearing a Tam o' Shanter and easy slippers. The consul dismounted and entered. The interior was simply, but tastefully furnished. It struck him that the Scotch prudence and economy, which practically excluded display and meretricious glitter, had reached the simplicity of the truest art and the most refined wealth. He felt he could understand Gray's enthusiasm, and by an odd association of ideas he found himself thinking of the resigned face of the lonely passenger on the Skyscraper.

"Have you heard any news of your friend who went to Rio?" he asked pleasantly, but without addressing himself particularly to either.

There was a perceptible pause; doubtless of deference to her father on the part of the young girl, and of the usual native conscientious caution on the part of the father, but neither betrayed any embarrassment or emotion. "No; he would not be writing yet," she at length said simply, "he would be waiting until he was settled to his business. Jamie would be waiting until he could say how he was doing, father?" she appealed interrogatively to the old man.

"Ay, James Gow would not fash himself to write compliments and gossip till he knew his position and work," corroborated the old man. "He'll not be going two thousand miles to send us what we can read in the 'St. Kentigern Herald.' But," he added, suddenly, with a recall of cautiousness, "perhaps YOU will be hearing of the ship?"

"The consul will not be remembering what he hears of all the ships," interposed the young girl, with the same gentle affectation of superior worldly knowledge which had before amused him. "We'll be wearying him, father," and the subject dropped.

The consul, glancing around the room again, but always returning to the sweet and patient seriousness of the young girl's face and the grave decorum of her father, would have liked to ask another question, but it was presently anticipated; for when he had exhausted the current topics, in which both father and daughter displayed a quiet sagacity, and he had gathered a sufficient knowledge of their character to seem to justify Gray's enthusiasm, and was rising to take his leave, the young girl said timidly:—

"Would ye not let Bessie take your horse to the grass field over yonder, and yourself stay with us to dinner? It would be most kind, and you would meet a great friend of yours who will be here."

"Mr. Gray?" suggested the consul audaciously. Yet he was greatly surprised when the young girl said quietly, "Ay."

"He'll be coming in the loch with his yacht," said the old man. "It's not so expensive lying here as at Bannock, I'm thinking; and the men cannot gang ashore for drink. Eh, but it's an awful waste o' pounds, shillings, and pence, keeping these gowks in idleness with no feeshin' nor carrying of passengers."

"Ay, but it's better Mr. Gray should pay them for being decent and well-behaved on board his ship, than that they should be out of work and rioting in taverns and lodging-houses. And you yourself, father, remember the herrin' fishers that come ashore at Ardie, and the deck hands of the excursion boat, and the language they'll be using."

"Have you had a cruise in the yacht?" asked the consul quickly.

"Ay," said the father, "we have been up and down the loch, and around the far point, but not for boardin' or lodgin' the night, nor otherwise conteenuing or parteeci-pating. I have explained to Mr. Gray that we must return to our own home and our own porridge at evening, and he has agreed, and even come with us. He's a decent enough lad, and not above instructin', but extraordinar' extravagant."

"Ye know, father," interposed the young girl, "he talks of fitting up the yacht for the fishing, and taking some of his most decent men on shares. He says he was very fond of fishing off the Massachusetts coast, in America. It will be, I'm thinking," she said, suddenly turning to the consul with an almost pathetic appeal in her voice, "a great occupation for the rich young men over there."

The consul, desperately struggling with a fanciful picture of Mr. Robert Gray as a herring fisher, thought gravely that it "might be." But he thought still more gravely, though silently, of this singular companion ship, and was somewhat anxious to confront his friend with his new acquaintances. He had not long to wait. The sun was just dipping behind the hill when the yacht glided into the lonely loch. A boat was put off, and in a few moments Robert Gray was climbing the little path from the loch.

Had the consul expected any embarrassment or lover-like consciousness on the face of Mr. Gray at their unexpected meeting, he would have been disappointed. Nor was the young man's greeting of father and daughter, whom he addressed as Mr. and Miss Callender, marked by any tenderness or hesitation. On the contrary, a certain seriousness and quiet reticence, unlike Gray, which might have been borrowed from his new friends, characterized his speech and demeanor. Beyond this freemasonry of sad repression there was no significance of look or word passed between these two young people. The girl's voice retained its even pathos. Gray's grave politeness was equally divided between her and her father. He corroborated what Callender had said of his previous visits without affectation or demonstration; he spoke of the possibilities of his fitting up the yacht for the fishing season with a practical detail and economy that left the consul's raillery ineffective. Even when, after dinner, the consul purposely walked out in the garden with the father, Gray and Ailsa presently followed them without lingering or undue precipitation, and with no change of voice or manner. The consul was perplexed. Had the girl already told Gray of her lover across the sea, and was this singular restraint their joint acceptance of their fate; or was he mistaken in supposing that their relations were anything more than the simple friendship of patron and protegee? Gray was rich enough to indulge in such a fancy, and the father and daughter were too proud to ever allow it to influence their own independence. In any event the consul's right to divulge the secret he was accidentally possessed of seemed more questionable than ever. Nor did there appear to be any opportunity for a confidential talk with Gray, since it was proposed that the whole party should return to the yacht for supper, after which the consul should be dropped at the pier-head, distant only a few minutes from his hotel, and his horse sent to him the next day.

A faint moon was shimmering along the surface of Loch Dour in icy little ripples when they pulled out from the shadows of the hillside. By the accident of position, Gray, who was steering, sat beside Ailsa in the stern, while the consul and Mr. Callender were further forward, although within hearing. The faces of the young people were turned towards each other, yet in the cold moonlight the consul fancied they looked as impassive and unemotional as statues. The few distant, far-spaced lights that trembled on the fading shore, the lonely glitter of the water, the blackness of the pine-clad ravines seemed to be a part of this repression, until the vast melancholy of the lake appeared to meet and overflow them like an advancing tide. Added to this, there came from time to time the faint sound and smell of the distant, desolate sea.

The consul, struggling manfully to keep up a spasmodic discussion on Scotch diminutives in names, found himself mechanically saying:

"And James you call Jamie?"

"Ay; but ye would say, to be pure Scotch, 'Hamish,'" said Mr. Callender precisely. The girl, however, had not spoken; but Gray turned to her with something of his old gayety.

"And I suppose you would call me 'Robbie'?"

"Ah, no!"

"What then?"

"Robin."

Her voice was low yet distinct, but she had thrown into the two syllables such infinite tenderness, that the consul was for an instant struck with an embarrassment akin to that he had felt in the cabin of the Skyscraper, and half expected the father to utter a shocked protest. And to save what he thought would be an appalling silence, he said with a quiet laugh:—

Bret Harte

"That's the fellow who 'made the assembly shine' in the song, isn't it?"

"That was Robin Adair," said Gray quietly; "unfortunately I would only be 'Robin Gray,' and that's quite another song."

"AULD Robin Gray, sir, deestinctly 'auld' in the song," interrupted Mr. Callender with stern precision; "and I'm thinking he was not so very unfortunate either."

The discussion of Scotch diminutives halting here, the boat sped on silently to the yacht. But although Robert Gray, as host, recovered some of his usual lightheartedness, the consul failed to discover anything in his manner to indicate the lover, nor did Miss Ailsa after her single lapse of tender accent exhibit the least consciousness. It was true that their occasional frank allusions to previous conversations seemed to show that their opportunities had not been restricted, but nothing more. He began again to think he was mistaken.

As he wished to return early, and yet not hasten the Callenders, he prevailed upon Gray to send him to the pier-head first, and not disturb the party. As he stepped into the boat, something in the appearance of the coxswain awoke an old association in his mind. The man at first seemed to avoid his scrutiny, but when they were well away from the yacht, he said hesitatingly:—

"I see you remember me, sir. But if it's all the same to you, I've got a good berth here and would like to keep it."

The consul had a flash of memory. It was the boatswain of the Skyscraper, one of the least objectionable of the crew. "But what are you doing here? you shipped for the voyage," he said sharply.

"Yes, but I got away at Key West, when I knew what was coming. I wasn't on her when she was abandoned."

"Abandoned!" repeated the consul. "What the d—l! Do you mean to say she was wrecked?"

"Well, yes—you know what I mean, sir. It was an understood thing. She was over-insured and scuttled in the Bahamas. It was a put-up job, and I reckoned I was well out of it."

"But there was a passenger! What of him?" demanded the consul anxiously.

"Dnnno! But I reckon he got away. There wasn't any of the crew lost that I know of. Let's see, he was an engineer, wasn't he? I reckon he had to take a hand at the pumps, and his chances with the rest."

"Does Mr. Gray know of this?" asked the consul after a pause.

The man stared.

"Not from me, sir. You see it was nothin' to him, and I didn't care talking much about the Skyscraper. It was hushed up in the papers. You won't go back on me, sir?"

"You don't know what became of the passenger?"

"No! But he was a Scotchman, and they're bound to fall on their feet somehow!"

III

The December fog that overhung St. Kentigern had thinned sufficiently to permit the passage of a few large snowflakes, soiled in their descent, until in color and consistency they spotted the steps of the Consulate and the umbrellas of the passers-by like sprinklings of gray mortar. Nevertheless the consul thought the streets preferable to the persistent gloom of his office, and sallied out. Youthful mercantile St. Kentigern strode sturdily past him in the lightest covert coats; collegiate St. Kentigern fluttered by in the scantiest of red gowns, shaming the furs that defended his more exotic blood; and the bare red feet of a few factory girls, albeit their heads and shoulders were draped and hooded in thick shawls, filled him with a keen sense of his effeminacy. Everything of earth, air, and sky, and even the faces of those he looked upon, seemed to be set in the hard, patient endurance of the race. Everywhere on that dismal day, he fancied he could see this energy without restlessness, this earnestness without geniality, all grimly set against the hard environment of circumstance and weather.

The consul turned into one of the main arteries of St. Kentigern, a wide street that, however, began and ended inconsequently, and with half a dozen social phases in as many blocks. Here the snow ceased, the fog thickened suddenly with the waning day, and the consul found himself isolated and cut off on a block which he did not remember, with the clatter of an invisible tramway in his ears. It was a block of small houses with smaller shopfronts. The one immediately before him seemed to be an optician's, but the dimly lighted windows also displayed the pathetic reinforcement of a few watches, cheap jewelry on cards, and several cairngorm brooches and pins set in silver. It occurred to him that he wanted a new watch crystal, and that he would procure it here and inquire his way. Opening the door he perceived that there was no one in the shop, but from behind the counter another open door disclosed a neat sitting-room, so close to the street that it gave the casual customer the sensation of having intruded upon domestic privacy. The consul's entrance tinkled a small bell which brought a figure to the door. It was Ailsa Callender.

The consul was startled. He had not seen her since he had brought to their cottage the news of the shipwreck with a precaution and delicacy that their calm self-control and patient resignation, however, seemed to make almost an impertinence. But this was no longer the handsome shop in the chief thoroughfare with its two shopmen, which he previously knew as "Callender's." And Ailsa here! What misfortune had befallen them

?Whatever it was, there was no shadow of it in her clear eyes and frank yet timid recognition of him. Falling in with her stoical and reticent acceptance of it, he nevertheless gathered that the Callenders had lost money in some invention which James Gow had taken with him to Rio, but which was sunk in the ship. With this revelation of a business interest in what he had believed was only a sentimental relation, the consul ventured to continue his inquiries. Mr. Gow had escaped with his life and had reached Honduras, where he expected to try his fortunes anew. It might be a year or two longer before there were any results. Did the consul know anything of Honduras? There was coffee there—so she and her father understood. All this with little hopefulness, no irritation, but a divine patience in her eyes. The consul, who found that his watch required extensive repairing, and had suddenly developed an inordinate passion for cairngorms, watched her as she opened the show-case with no affectation of unfamiliarity with her occupation, but with all her old serious concern. Surely she would have made as thorough a shop-girl as she would—His half-formulated thought took the shape of a question.

"Have you seen Mr. Gray since his return from the Mediterranean?"

Ah! one of the brooches had slipped from her fingers to the bottom of the case. There was an interval or two of pathetic murmuring, with her fair head under the glass, before she could find it; then she lifted her eyes to the consul. They were still slightly suffused with her sympathetic concern. The stone, which was set in a thistle—the national emblem—did he not know it?—had dropped out. But she could put it in. It was pretty and not expensive. It was marked twelve shillings on the card, but he could have it for ten shillings. No, she had not seen Mr. Gray since they had lost their fortune. (It struck the consul as none the less pathetic that she seemed really to believe in their former opulence.) They could not be seeing him there in a small shop, and they could not see him elsewhere. It was far better as it was. Yet she paused a moment when she had wrapped up the brooch. "You'd be seeing him yourself some time?" she added gently.

"Perhaps."

"Then you'll not mind saying how my father and myself are sometimes thinking of his goodness and kindness," she went on, in a voice whose tenderness seemed to increase with the formal precision of her speech.

"Certainly."

"And you'll say we're not forgetting him."

"I promise."

As she handed him the parcel her lips softly parted in what might have been equally a smile or a sigh.

He was able to keep his promise sooner than he had imagined. It was only a few weeks later that, arriving in London, he found Gray's hatbox and bag in the vestibule of his club, and that gentleman himself in the smoking-room. He looked tanned and older.

"I only came from Southampton an hour ago, where I left the yacht. And," shaking the consul's hand cordially, "how's everything and everybody up at old St. Kentigern?"

The consul thought fit to include his news of the Callenders in reference to that query, and with his eyes fixed on Gray dwelt at some length on their change of fortune. Gray took his cigar from his mouth, but did not lift his eyes from the fire. Presently he said, "I suppose that's why Callender declined to take the shares I offered him in the fishing scheme. You know I meant it, and would have done it."

"Perhaps he had other reasons."

"What do you mean?" said Gray, facing the consul suddenly.

"Look here, Gray," said the consul, "did Miss Callender or her father ever tell you she was engaged?"

"Yes; but what's that to do with it?"

"A good deal. Engagements, you know, are sometimes forced, unsuitable, or unequal, and are broken by circumstances. Callender is proud."

Gray turned upon the consul the same look of gravity that he had worn on the yacht—the same look that the consul even fancied he had seen in Ailsa's eyes. "That's exactly where you're mistaken in her," he said slowly. "A girl like that gives her word and keeps it. She waits, hopes, accepts what may come—breaks her heart, if you will, but not her word. Come, let's talk of something else. How did he—that man Gow—lose Callender's money?"

The consul did not see the Callenders again on his return, and perhaps did not think it necessary to report the meeting. But one morning he was delighted to find an official document from New York upon his desk, asking him to communicate with David Callender of St. Kentigern, and, on proof of his identity, giving him authority to draw the sum of five thousand dollars damages awarded for the loss of certain property on the Skyscraper, at the request of James Gow. Yet it was with mixed sensations that the consul sought the little shop of the optician with this convincing proof of Gow's faithfulness and the indissolubility of Ailsa's engagement. That there was some sad understanding between the girl and Gray he did not doubt, and perhaps it was not strange that he felt a slight partisanship for his friend, whose nature had so strangely changed. Miss Ailsa was not there. Her father explained that her health had required a change, and she was visiting some friends on the river.

"I'm thinkin' that the atmosphere is not so pure here. It is deficient in ozone. I noticed it myself in the early morning. No! it was not the confinement of the shop, for she never cared to go out."

He received the announcement of his good fortune with unshaken calm and great practical consideration of detail. He would guarantee his identity to the consul. As for James Gow, it was no more than fair; and what he had expected of him. As to its being an equivalent of his loss, he could not tell until the facts were before him.

"Miss Ailsa," suggested the consul venturously, "will be pleased to hear again from her old friend, and know that he is succeeding."

"I'm not so sure that ye could call it 'succeeding,'" returned the old man, carefully wiping the glasses of a pair of spectacles that he held critically to the light, "when ye consider that, saying nothing of the waste of valuable time, it only puts James Gow back where he was when he went away."

"But any man who has had the pleasure of knowing Mr. and Miss Callender would be glad to be on that footing," said the consul, with polite significance.

"I'm not agreeing with you there," said Mr. Callender quietly; "and I'm observing in ye of late a tendency to combine business wi' compleement. But it was kind of ye to call; and I'll be sending ye the authorization."

Which he did. But the consul, passing through the locality a few weeks later, was somewhat concerned to find the shop closed, with others on the same block, behind a hoarding that indicated rebuilding and improvement. Further inquiry elicited the fact that the small leases had been bought up by some capitalist, and that Mr. Callender, with the others, had benefited thereby. But there was no trace nor clew to his present locality. He and his daughter seemed to have again vanished with this second change in their fortunes.

It was a late March morning when the streets were dumb with snow, and the air was filled with flying granulations that tinkled against the windows of the Consulate like fairy sleigh-bells, when there was the stamping of snow-clogged feet in the outer hall, and the door was opened to Mr. and Miss Callender. For an instant the consul was startled. The old man appeared as usual—erect, and as frigidly respectable as one of the icicles that fringed the window, but Miss Ailsa was, to his astonishment, brilliant with a new-found color, and sparkling with health and only half-repressed animation. The snow-flakes, scarcely melting on the brown head of this true daughter of the North, still crowned her hood; and, as she threw back her brown cloak and disclosed a plump little scarlet jacket and brown skirt, the consul could not resist her suggested likeness to some bright-eyed robin redbreast, to whom the inclement weather had given a charming audacity. And shy and demure as she still was, it was evident that some change had been wrought in her other than that evoked by the stimulus of her native sky and air.

To his eager questioning, the old man replied briefly that he had bought the old cottage at Loch Dour, where they were living, and where he had erected a small manufactory and laboratory for the making of his inventions, which had become profitable. The consul reiterated his delight at meeting them again.

"I'm not so sure of that, sir, when you know the business on which I come," said Mr. Callender, dropping rigidly into a chair, and clasping his hands over the crutch of a shepherd-like staff. "Ye mind, perhaps, that ye conveyed to me, ostensibly at the request of James Gow, a certain sum of money, for which I gave ye a good and sufficient guarantee. I thought at the time that it was a most feckless and unbusiness-like proceeding on the part of James, as it was without corroboration or advice by letter; but I took the money."

"Do you mean to say that he made no allusion to it in his other letters?" interrupted the consul, glancing at Ailsa.

"There were no other letters at the time," said Callender dryly. "But about a month afterwards we DID receive a letter from him enclosing a draft and a full return of the profits of the invention, which HE HAD SOLD IN HONDURAS. Ye'll observe the deescrepancy! I then wrote to the bank on which I had drawn as you authorized me, and I found that they knew nothing of any damages awarded, but that the sum I had drawn had been placed to my credit by Mr. Robert Gray."

In a flash the consul recalled the one or two questions that Gray had asked him, and saw it all. For an instant he felt the whole bitterness of Gray's misplaced generosity—its exposure and defeat. He glanced again hopelessly at Ailsa. In the eye of that fresh, glowing, yet demure, young goddess, unhallowed as the thought might be, there was certainly a distinctly tremulous wink.

The consul took heart. "I believe I need not say, Mr. Callender," he began with some stiffness, "that this is as great a surprise to me as to you. I had no reason to believe the transaction other than bona fide, and acted accordingly. If my friend, deeply sympathizing with your previous misfortune, has hit upon a delicate, but unbusiness-like way of assisting you temporarily—I say TEMPORARILY, because it must have been as patent to him as to you, that you would eventually find out his generous deceit—you surely can forgive him for the sake of his kind intention. Nay, more; may I point out to you that you have no right to assume that this benefaction was intended exclusively for you; if Mr. Gray, in his broader sympathy with you and your daughter, has in this way chosen to assist and strengthen the position of a gentleman so closely connected with you, but still struggling with hard fortune"—

"I'd have ye know, sir," interrupted the old man, rising to his feet, "that ma frien' Mr. James Gow is as independent of yours as he is of me and mine. He has married, sir, a Mrs. Hernandez, the rich widow of a coffee-planter, and now is the owner of the whole estate, minus the encumbrance of three children. And now, sir, you'll take this,"—he drew from his pocket an envelope. "It's a draft for five thousand dollars, with the ruling rate of interest computed from the day I received it till this day, and ye'll give it to your frien' when ye see him. And ye'll just say to him from me"—

But Miss Ailsa, with a spirit and independence that challenged her father's, here suddenly fluttered between them with sparkling eyes and outstretched hands.

"And ye'll say to him from ME that a more honorable, noble, and generous man, and a kinder, truer, and better friend than he, cannot be found anywhere! And that the foolishest and most extravagant thing he ever did is better than the wisest and most prudent thing that anybody else ever did, could, or would do! And if he was a bit overproud—it was only because those about him were overproud and foolish. And you'll tell him that we're wearying for him! And when you give him that daft letter from father you'll give him this bit line from me," she went on rapidly as she laid a tiny note in his hand. "And," with wicked dancing eyes that seemed to snap the last bond of repression, "ye'll give him THAT too, and say I sent it!"

There was a stir in the official apartment! The portraits of Lincoln and Washington rattled uneasily in their frames; but it was no doubt only a discreet blast of the north wind that drowned the echo of a kiss.

"Ailsa!" gasped the shocked Mr. Callender.

"Ah! but, father, if it had not been for HIM we would not have known Robin."

*****

It was the last that the consul saw of Ailsa Callender; for the next summer when he called at Loch Dour she was Mrs. Gray.

THE SHERIFF OF SISKYOU

I

On the fifteenth of August, 1854, what seemed to be the entire population of Wynyard's Bar was collected upon a little bluff which overlooked the rude wagon road that was the only approach to the settlement. In general appearance the men differed but little from ordinary miners, although the foreign element, shown in certain Spanish peculiarities of dress and color, predominated, and some of the men were further distinguished by the delicacy of education and sedentary pursuits. Yet Wynyard's Bar was a city of refuge, comprised among its inhabitants a number who were "wanted" by the State authorities, and its actual attitude at that moment was one of open rebellion against the legal power, and of particular resistance to the apprehension by warrant of one of its prominent members. This gentleman, Major Overstone, then astride of a gray mustang, and directing the movements of the crowd, had, a few days before, killed the sheriff of Siskyou county, who had attempted to arrest him for the double offense of misappropriating certain corporate funds of the State and the shooting of the editor who had imprudently exposed him. The lesser crime of homicide might have been overlooked by the authorities, but its repetition upon the body of their own over-zealous and misguided official could not pass unchallenged if they expected to arrest Overstone for the more serious offense against property. So it was known that a new sheriff had been appointed and was coming to Wynyard's Bar with an armed posse. But it was also understood that this invasion would be resisted by the Bar to its last man.

All eyes were turned upon a fringe of laurel and butternut that encroached upon the road half a mile away, where it seemed that such of the inhabitants who were missing from the bluff were hidden to give warning or retard the approach of the posse. A gray haze, slowly rising between the fringe and the distant hillside, was recognized as the dust of a cavalcade passing along the invisible highway. In the hush of expectancy that followed, the irregular clatter of hoofs, the sharp crack of a rifle, and a sudden halt were faintly audible. The men, scattered in groups on the bluff, exchanged a smile of grim satisfaction.

Not so their leader! A quick start and an oath attracted attention to him. To their surprise he was looking in another direction, but as they looked too they saw and understood the cause. A file of horsemen, hitherto undetected, were slowly passing along the little ridge on their right. Their compact accoutrements and the yellow braid on their blue jackets, distinctly seen at that distance, showed them to be a detachment of United States cavalry.

Before the assemblage could realize this new invasion, a nearer clatter of hoofs was heard along the high road, and one of the ambuscading party dashed up from the fringe of woods below. His face was flushed, but triumphant.

"A reg'lar skunk—by the living hokey!" he panted,

pointing to the faint haze that was again slowly rising above the invisible road. "They backed down as soon as they saw our hand, and got a hole through their new sheriff's hat. But what are you lookin' at? What's up?"

The leader impatiently pointed with a darkening face to the distant file.

"Reg'lars, by gum!" ejaculated the other. "But Uncle Sam ain't in this game. Wot right have THEY"—

"Dry up!" said the leader.

The detachment was now moving at right angles with the camp, but suddenly halted, almost doubling upon itself in some evident commotion. A dismounted figure was seen momentarily flying down the hillside dodging from bush to bush until lost in the underbrush. A dozen shots were fired over its head, and then the whole detachment wheeled and came clattering down the trail in the direction of the camp. A single riderless horse, evidently that of the fugitive, followed.

"Spread yourselves along the ridge, every man of you, and cover them as they enter the gulch!" shouted the leader. "But not a shot until I give the word. Scatter!"

The assemblage dispersed like a startled village of prairie dogs, squatting behind every available bush and rock along the line of bluff. The leader alone trotted quietly to the head of the gulch.

The nine cavalrymen came smartly up in twos, a young officer leading. The single figure of Major Overstone opposed them with a command to halt. Looking up, the young officer drew rein, said a word to his file leader, and the four files closed in a compact square motionless on the road. The young officer's unsworded hand hung quietly at his thigh, the men's unslung carbines rested easily on their saddles. Yet at that moment every man of them knew that they were covered by a hundred rifles and shot guns leveled from every bush, and that they were caught helplessly in a trap.

"Since when," said Major Overstone with an affectation of tone and manner different from that in which he had addressed his previous companions, "have the Ninth United States Cavalry helped to serve a State court's pettifogging process?"

"We are hunting a deserter—a half-breed agent—who has just escaped us," returned the officer. His voice was boyish—so, too, was his figure in its slim, cadet-like smartness of belted tunic—but very quiet and level, although his face was still flushed with the shock and shame of his surprise.

The relaxation of relief went through the wrought and waiting camp. The soldiers were not seeking THEM. Ready as these desperate men had been to do their leader's bidding, they were well aware that a momentary victory over the troopers would not pass unpunished, and meant the ultimate dispersion of the camp. And quiet as these innocent invaders seemed to be they would no doubt sell their lives dearly. The embattled desperadoes glanced anxiously at their leader; the soldiers, on the contrary, looked straight before them.

"Process or no process," said Major Overstone with a sneer, "you've come to the last place to recover your deserter. We don't give up men in Wynyard's Bar. And they didn't teach you at the Academy, sir, to stop to take

Bret Harte

prisoners when you were outflanked and outnumbered."

"Bedad! They didn't teach YOU, Captain Overstone, to engage a battery at Cerro Gordo with a half company, but you did it; more shame to you now, sorr, commandin' the thayves and ruffians you do."

"Silence!" said the young officer.

The sleeve of the sergeant who had spoken—with the chevrons of long service upon it—went up to a salute, and dropped again over his carbine as he stared stolidly before him. But his shot had told. A flush of mingled pride and shame passed over Overstone's face.

"Oh! it's YOU, Murphy," he said with an affected laugh, "and you haven't improved with your stripes."

The young officer turned his head slightly.

"Attention!"

"One moment more," said Overstone coming forward. "I have told you that we don't give up any man who seeks our protection. But," he added with a half-careless, half-contemptuous wave of his hand, and a significant glance at his followers, "we don't prevent you from seeking him. The road is clear; the camp is before you."

The young officer continued without looking at him. "Forward—in two files—open order. Ma-arch!"

The little troop moved forward, passed Major Overstone at the head of the gully, and spread out on the hillside. The assembled camp, still armed, lounging out of ambush here and there, ironically made way for them to pass. A few moments of this farcical quest, and a glance at the impenetrably wooded heights around, apparently satisfied the young officer, and he turned his files again into the gully. Major Overstone was still lingering there.

"I hope you are satisfied," he said grimly. He then paused, and in a changed and more hesitating voice added: "I am an older soldier than you, sir, but I am always glad to make the acquaintance of West Point." He paused and held out his hand.

West Point, still red and rigid, glanced at him with bright clear eyes under light lashes and the peak of a smartly cocked cap, looked coolly at the proffered hand, raised his own to a stiff salute, said, "Good afternoon, sir," and rode away.

Major Overstone wheeled angrily, but in doing so came sharply upon his coadjutor—the leader of the ambushed party.

"Well, Dawson," he said impatiently. "Who was it?"

"Only one of them d—d half-breed Injin agents. He's just over there in the brush with Simpson, lying low till the soldiers clear out."

"Did you talk to him?"

"Not much!" returned Dawson scornfully. "He ain't my style."

"Fetch him up to my cabin; he may be of some use to us."

Dawson looked skeptical. "I reckon he ain't no more gain here than he was over there," he said, and turned away.

Bret Harte

II

The cabin of Major Overstone differed outwardly but little from those of his companions. It was the usual structure of logs, laid lengthwise, and rudely plastered at each point of contact with adobe, the material from which the chimney, which entirely occupied one gable, was built. It was pierced with two windows and a door, roofed with smaller logs, and thatched with long half cylinders of spruce bark. But the interior gave certain indications of the distinction as well as the peculiar experiences of its occupant. In place of the usual bunk or berth built against the wall stood a small folding camp bedstead, and upon a rude deal table that held a tin wash-basin and pail lay two ivory-handled brushes, combs, and other elegant toilet articles, evidently the contents of the major's dressing-bag. A handsome leather trunk occupied one corner, with a richly caparisoned silver-mounted Mexican saddle, a mahogany case of dueling pistols, a leather hat-box, locked and strapped, and a gorgeous gold and quartz handled ebony "presentation" walking stick. There was a certain dramatic suggestion in this revelation of the sudden and hurried transition from a life of ostentatious luxury to one of hidden toil and privation, and a further significance in the slow and gradual distribution and degradation of these elegant souvenirs. A pair of silver boot-hooks had been used for raking the hearth and lifting the coffee kettle; the ivory of the brushes was stained with coffee; the cut-glass bottles had lost their stoppers, and had been utilized for vinegar and salt; a silver-framed hand mirror hung against the blackened wall. For the major's occupancy was the sequel of a hurried flight from his luxurious hotel at Sacramento—a transfer that he believed was only temporary until the affair blew over, and he could return in safety to brow-beat his accusers, as was his wont. But this had not been so easy as he had imagined; his prosecutors were bitter, and his enforced seclusion had been prolonged week by week until the fracas which ended in the shooting of the sheriff had apparently closed the door upon his return to civilization forever. Only here was his life and person secure. For Wynyard's Bar had quickly succumbed to the domination of his reckless courage, and the eminence of his double crime had made him respected among spendthrifts, gamblers, and gentlemen whose performances had never risen above a stage-coach robbery or a single assassination. Even criticism of his faded luxuries had been delicately withheld.

He was leaning over his open trunk—which the camp popularly supposed to contain State bonds and securities of fabulous amount—and had taken some letters from it, when a figure darkened the doorway. He looked up, laying his papers carelessly aside. WITHIN Wynyard's Bar property was sacred.

It was the late fugitive. Although some hours had already elapsed since his arrival in camp, and he had presumably refreshed himself inwardly, his outward appearance was still disheveled and dusty. Brier and milkweed clung to his frayed blouse and trousers. What could be seen of the skin of his face and hands under its stains and begriming was of a dull yellow. His light eyes had all the brightness without the restlessness of the mongrel race. They leisurely took in the whole cabin, the still open trunk before the major, and then rested deliberately on the major himself.

"Well," said Major Overstone abruptly, "what brought you here?"

"Same as brought you, I reckon," responded the man almost as abruptly.

The major knew something of the half-breed temper, and neither the retort nor its tone affected him.

"You didn't come here just because you deserted," said the major coolly. "You've been up to something else."

"I have," said the man with equal coolness.

"I thought so. Now, you understand you can't try anything of that kind HERE. If you do, up you go on the first tree. That's Rule 1."

"I see you ain't pertickler about waiting for the sheriff here, you fellers."

The major glanced at him quickly. He seemed to be quite unconscious of any irony in his remark, and continued grimly, "And what's Rule 2?"

"I reckon you needn't trouble yourself beyond No. 1," returned the major with dry significance. Nevertheless, he opened a rude cupboard in the corner and brought out a rich silver-mounted cut-glass drinking-flask, which he handed to the stranger.

"I say," said the half-breed, admiringly, "yours?"

"Certainly."

"Certainly NOW, but BEFORE, eh?"

Rule No. 2 may have indicated that references to the past held no dishonor. The major, although accustomed to these pleasantries, laughed a little harshly.

"Mine always," he said. "But you don't drink?"

The half-breed's face darkened under its grime.

"Wot you're givin' us? I've been filled chock up by Simpson over thar. I reckon I know when I've got a load on."

"Were you ever in Sacramento?"

"Yes."

"When?"

"Last week."

"Did you hear anything about me?"

The half-breed glanced through his tangled hair at the major in some wonder, not only at the question, but at the almost childish eagerness with which it was asked.

"I didn't hear much of anything else," he answered grimly.

"And—what did they SAY?"

"Said you'd got to be TOOK anyhow! They allowed the new sheriff would do it too."

The major laughed. "Well, you heard HOW the new sheriff did it—skunked away with his whole posse before one-eighth of my men! You saw how the rest of this camp held up your nine troopers, and that sap-headed cub of a lieutenant—didn't you? You wouldn't have been standing here if you hadn't. No; there isn't the civil process nor the civil power in all California that can take me out of this camp."

But neither his previous curiosity nor present bravado seemed to impress the ragged stranger with much favor. He glanced sulkily around the cabin and began to shuffle towards the door.

"Stop! Where are you going to? Sit down. I want to talk to you."

The fugitive hesitated for a moment, and then dropped ungraciously on the edge of a camp-stool near the door. The major looked at him.

"I may have to remind you that I run this camp, and the boys hereabouts do pretty much as I say. What's your name?"

"Tom."

"Tom? Well, look here, Tom! D—n it all! Can't you see that when a man is stuck here alone, as I am, he wants to know what's going on outside, and hear a little fresh talk?"

The singular weakness of this blended command and appeal apparently struck the fugitive curiously. He fixed his lowering eyes on the major as if in gloomy doubt if he were really the reckless desperado he had been represented. That this man—twice an assassin and the ruler of outlaws as reckless as himself—should approach him in this half-confidential way evidently puzzled him.

"Wot you wanter know?" he asked gruffly.

"Well, what's my party saying or doing about me?" said the major impatiently. "What's the 'Express' saying about me?"

"I reckon they're throwing off on you all round; they allow you never represented the party, but worked for yourself," said the man shortly.

Here the major lashed out. A set of traitors and hirelings! He had bought and paid for them all! He had sunk two thousand dollars in the "Express" and saved the editor from being horsewhipped and jailed for libel! Half the cursed bonds that they were making such a blanked fuss about were handled by these hypocrites—blank them! They were a low-lived crew of thieves and deserters! It is presumed that the major had forgotten himself in this infelicitous selection of epithets, but the stranger's face only relaxed into a grim smile. More than that, the major had apparently forgotten his desire to hear his guest talk, for he himself at once launched into an elaborate exposition of his own affairs and a specious and equally elaborate defense and justification of himself and denunciation of his accusers. For nearly half an hour he reviewed step by step and detail by detail the charges against him—with plausible explanation and sophistical argument, but always with a singular prolixity and reiteration that spoke of incessant self-consciousness and self-abstraction. Of that dashing self-sufficiency which had dazzled his friends and awed his enemies there was no trace! At last, even the set smile of the degraded recipient of these confidences darkened with a dull, bewildered disgust. Then, to his relief, a step was heard without. The major's manner instantly changed.

"Well?" he demanded impatiently, as Dawson entered.

"I came to know what you want done with HIM," said Dawson, indicating the fugitive with a contemptuous finger.

"Take him to your cabin!"

"My cabin! HIM?" ejaculated Dawson, turning sharply on his chief.

The major's light eyes contracted and his thin lips became a straight line. "I don't think you understand me, Dawson, and another time you'd better wait until I'm done. I want you to take him to your cabin—and then CLEAR OUT OF IT YOURSELF. You understand? I want him NEAR ME AND ALONE!"

III

Dawson was not astonished the next morning to see Major Overstone and the half-breed walking together down the gully road, for he had already come to the conclusion that the major was planning some extraordinary reprisals against the invaders, that would ensure the perpetual security of the camp. That he should use so insignificant and unimportant a tool now appeared to him to be quite natural, particularly as the service was probably one in which the man would be sacrificed. "The major," he suggested to his companions, "ain't going to risk a white man's skin, when he can get an Injun's hide handy."

The reluctant hesitating step of the half-breed as they walked along seemed to give some color to this hypothesis. He listened sullenly to the major as he pointed out the strategic position of the Bar. "That wagon road is the only approach to Wynyard's, and a dozen men along the rocks could hold it against a hundred. The trail that you came by, over the ridge, drops straight into this gully, and you saw what that would mean to any blanked fools who might try it. Of course we could be shelled from that ridge if the sheriff had a howitzer, or the men who knew how to work one, but even then we could occupy the ridge before them." He paused a moment and then added: "I used to be in the army, Tom; I saw service in Mexico before that cub you got away from had his first trousers. I was brought up as a gentleman—blank it all—and HERE I am!"

The man slouched on by his side, casting his surly, furtive glances from left to right, as if seeking to escape from these confidences. Nevertheless, the major kept on through the gully, until reaching the wagon road they crossed it, and began to ascend the opposite slope, half hidden by the underbrush and larches. Here the major paused again and faced about. The cabins of the settlement were already behind the bluff; the little stream which indicated the "bar"—on which some perfunctory mining was still continued—now and then rang out quite clearly at their feet, although the bar itself had disappeared. The sounds of occupation and labor had at last died away in the distance. They were quite alone. The major sat down on a boulder, and pointed to another. The man, however, remained sullenly standing where he was, as if to accent as strongly as possible the enforced companionship. Either the major was too self-absorbed to notice it, or accepted it as a satisfactory characteristic of the half-breed's race. He continued confidently:—

"Now look here, Tom. I want to leave this cursed hole, and get clear out of the State! Anywhere; over the Oregon line into British Columbia, or to the coast, where I can get a coasting vessel down to Mexico. It will cost money, but I've got it. It will cost a lot of risks, but I'll take them. I want somebody to help me, some one to share risks with me, and some one to share my luck if I succeed. Help to put me on the other side of the border line, by sea or land, and I'll give you a thousand dollars down BEFORE WE START and a thousand dollars when I'm safe."

The half-breed had changed his slouching attitude. It seemed more indolent on account of the loosely hanging strap that had once held his haversack, which was still worn in a slovenly fashion over his shoulder as a kind of lazy sling for his shiftless hand.

"Well, Tom, is it a go? You can trust ME, for you'll have the thousand in your pocket before you start. I can trust

YOU, for I'll kill you quicker than lightning if you say a word of this to any one before I go, or play a single trick on me afterwards."

Suddenly the two men were rolling over and over in the underbrush. The half-breed had thrown himself upon the major, bearing him down to the ground. The haversack strap for an instant whirled like the loop of a lasso in the air, and descended over the major's shoulders, pinioning his arms to his side. Then the half-breed, tearing open his ragged blouse, stripped off his waist-belt, and as dexterously slipped it over the ankles of the struggling man.

It was all over in a moment. Neither had spoken a word. Only their rapid panting broke the profound silence. Each probably knew that no outcry would be overheard.

For the first time the half-breed sat down. But there was no trace of triumph or satisfaction in his face, which wore the same lowering look of disgust, as he gazed upon the prostrate man.

"I want to tell you first," he said, slowly wiping his face, "that I didn't kalkilate upon doin' this in this yer kind o' way. I expected more of a stan' up fight from you—more risk in gettin' you out o' that hole—and a different kind of a man to tackle. I never expected you to play into my hand like this—and it goes against me to hev to take advantage of it."

"Who are you?" said the major, pantingly.

"I'm the new sheriff of Siskyou!"

He drew from beneath his begrimed shirt a paper

wrapping, from which he gingerly extracted with the ends of his dirty fingers a clean, legal-looking folded paper.

"That's my warrant! I've kept it fresh for you. I reckon you don't care to read it—you've seen it afore. It's just the same as t'other sheriff had—what you shot."

"Then this was a plant of yours, and that whelp's troopers?" said the major.

"Neither him nor the sojers knows any more about it than you," returned the sheriff slowly. "I enlisted as Injin guide or scout ten days ago. I deserted just as reg'lar and nat'ral like when we passed that ridge yesterday. I could be took to-morrow by the sojers if they caught sight o' me and court-martialed—it's as reg'lar as THAT! But I timed to have my posse, under a deputy, draw you off by an attack just as the escort reached the ridge. And here I am."

"And you're no half-breed?"

"There's nothin' Injin about me that water won't wash off. I kalkilated you wouldn't suspect anything so insignificant as an INJIN, when I fixed myself up. You saw Dawson didn't hanker after me much. But I didn't reckon on YOUR tumbling to me so quick. That's what gets me! You must hev been pretty low down for kempany when you took a man like me inter your confidence. I don't see it yet."

He looked inquiringly at his captive—with the same wondering surliness. Nor could he understand another thing which was evident. After the first shock of resistance the major had exhibited none of the indignation of a betrayed man, but actually seemed to accept the situation with a calmness that his captor lacked. His voice was quite unemotional as he said:

"And how are you going to get me away from here?"

"That's MY look out, and needn't trouble you, major; but, seen' as how confidential you've been to me, I don't mind tellin' you. Last night that posse of mine that you 'skunked,' you know, halted at the cross roads till them sojers went by. They has only to SEE THEM to know that I had got away. They'll hang round the cross roads till they see my signal on top of the ridge, and then they'll make another show against that pass. Your men will have their hands full, I reckon, without huntin' for YOU, or noticin' the three men o' mine that will come along this ridge where the sojers come yesterday—to help me get you down in the same way. You see, major, your little trap in that gully ain't in this fight—WE'RE THE OTHER SIDE OF IT. I ain't much of a sojer, but I reckon I've got you there! And it's all owing to YOU. I ain't," he added gloomily, "takin' much pride in it MYSELF."

"I shouldn't think you would," said the major, "and look here! I'll double that offer I made you just now. Set me down just as I am on the deck of some coasting vessel, and I'll pay you four thousand dollars. You may have all the glory of having captured me, HERE, and of making your word good before your posse. But you can arrange afterwards on the way to let me give you the slip somewhere near Sacramento."

The sheriff's face actually brightened. "Thanks for that, major. I was gettin' a little sick of my share in this job, but, by God, you've put some sand in me. Well, then! there ain't gold enough in all Californy to make me let you go. You hear me; so drop that. I've TOOK you, and TOOK ye'll remain until I land you in Sacramento jail. I don't want to kill you, though your life's forfeit a dozen times over, and I reckon you don't care for it either way, but if you try any tricks on me I may have to MAIM ye to make you come along comf'able and easy. I ain't hankerin' arter THAT either, but come you shall!"

"Give your signal and have an end of this," said the major curtly.

The sheriff looked at him again curiously. "I never had my hands in another man's pockets before, major, but I reckon I'll have to take your derringers from yours." He slipped his hand into the major's waistcoat and secured the weapons. "I'll have to trouble you for your sash, too," he said, unwinding the knitted silken girdle from the captive's waist. "You won't want it, for you ain't walking, and it'll come in handy to me just now."

He bent over, and, passing it across the major's breast with more gentleness and solicitude than he had yet shown, secured him in an easy sitting posture against the tree. Then, after carefully trying the knots and straps that held his prisoner, he turned and lightly bounded up the hill.

He was absent scarcely ten minutes, yet when he returned the major's eyes were half closed. But not his lips. "If you expect to hold me until your posse comes you had better take me to some less exposed position," he said dryly. "There's a man just crossed the gully, coming into the brush below in the wood."

"None of your tricks, major!"

"Look for yourself."

The sheriff glanced quickly below him. A man with an axe on his shoulder could be seen plainly making his way through the underbrush not a hundred yards away. The sheriff instantly clapped his hand upon his captive's mouth, but at a look from his eyes took it away again.

"I see," he said grimly, "you don't want to lure that man within reach of my revolver by calling to him."

"I could have called him while you were away," returned the major quietly.

The sheriff with a darkened face loosened the sash that bound his prisoner to the tree, and then, lifting him in his arms, began to ascend the hill cautiously, dipping into the heavier shadows. But the ascent was difficult, the load a heavy one, and the sheriff was agile rather than muscular. After a few minutes' climbing he was forced to pause and rest his burden at the foot of a tree. But the valley and the man in the underbrush were no longer in view.

"Come," said the major quietly, "unstrap my ankles and I'll WALK up. We'll never get there at this rate."

The sheriff paused, wiped his grimy face with his grimier blouse, and stood looking at his prisoner. Then he said slowly:—

"Look yer! Wot's your little game? Blessed if I kin follow suit."

For the first time the major burst into a rage. "Blast it all! Don't you see that if I'm discovered HERE, in this way, there's not a man on the Bar who would believe that I walked into your trap, not a man, by God, who wouldn't think it was a trick of yours and mine together?"

"Or," interrupted the sheriff slowly, fixing his eyes on his prisoner, "not a man who would ever trust Major Overstone for a leader again?"

"Perhaps," said the major, unmovedly again, "I don't think EITHER OF US would ever get a chance of being trusted again by any one."

The sheriff still kept his eyes fixed on his prisoner, his gloomy face growing darker under its grime. "THAT ain't the reason, major. Life and death don't mean much more to you than they do to me in this yer game. I know that you'd kill me quicker nor lightning if you got the chance; YOU know that I'm takin' you to the gallows."

"The reason is that I want to leave Wynyard's Bar," said the major coolly; "and even this way out of it will suit me."

The sheriff took his revolver from his pocket and deliberately cocked it. Then, leaning down, he unbuckled the strap from the major's ankles. A wild hope that his incomprehensible captive might seize that moment to develop his real intent—that he might fly, fight, or in some way act up to his reckless reputation—sustained him for a moment, but in the next proved futile. The major only said, "Thank you, Tom," and stretched his cramped legs.

"Get up and go on," said the sheriff roughly.

The major began to slowly ascend the hill, the sheriff close on his heels, alert, tingling, and watchful of every movement. For a few moments this strain upon his faculties seemed to invigorate him, and his gloom relaxed, but presently it became too evident that the prisoner's pinioned arms made it impossible for him to balance or help himself on that steep trail, and once or twice he stumbled and reeled dangerously to one side. With an oath the sheriff caught him, and tore from his arms the only remaining bonds that fettered him. "There!" he said savagely; "go on; we're equal!"

Without replying, the major continued his ascent; it became steeper as they neared the crest, and at last they were both obliged to drag themselves up by clutching the vines and underbrush. Suddenly the major stopped with a listening gesture. A strange roaring—as of wind or water—was distinctly audible.

"How did you signal?" asked the major abruptly.

"Made a smoke," said the sheriff as abruptly.

"I thought so—well! you've set the woods on fire."

They both plunged upwards again, now quite abreast, vying with each other to reach the summit as if with the one thought only. Already the sting and smart of acrid fumes were in their eyes and nostrils; when they at last stood on level ground again, it was hidden by a thin film of grayish blue haze that seemed to be creeping along it. But above was the clear sky, seen through the interlacing boughs, and to their surprise—they who had just come from the breathless, stagnant hillside—a fierce wind was blowing! But the roaring was louder than before.

"Unless your three men are already here, your game is up," said the major calmly. "The wind blows dead along the ridge where they should come, and they can't get through the smoke and fire."

It was indeed true! In the scarce twenty minutes that had elapsed since the sheriff's return the dry and brittle underbrush for half a mile on either side had been converted into a sheet of flame, which at times rose to a furnace blast through the tall chimney-like conductors of tree shafts, from whose shriveled sides bark was crackling, and lighted dead limbs falling in all directions. The whole valley, the gully, the Bar, the very hillside they had just left, were blotted out by a creeping, stifling smoke-fog that scarcely rose breast high, but was beaten down or cut off cleanly by the violent wind that swept the higher level of the forest. At times this gale became a sirocco in temperature, concentrating its heat in withering blasts which they could not face, or focusing its intensity upon some mass of foliage that seemed to shrink at its touch and open a scathed and quivering aisle to its approach. The enormous skeleton of a dead and rotten redwood, not a hundred yards to their right, broke suddenly like a gigantic firework into sparks and flame.

The sheriff had grasped the full meaning of their situation. In spite of his first error—the very carelessness of familiarity—his knowledge of woodcraft was greater than his companion's, and he saw their danger. "Come," he said quickly, "we must make for an opening or we shall be caught."

The major smiled in misapprehension.

"Who could catch us here?"

The sheriff pointed to the blazing tree.

"THAT," he said. "In five minutes IT will have a posse that will wipe us both out."

He caught the major by the arm and rushed him into the smoke, apparently in the direction of the greatest mass of flame. The heat was suffocating, but it struck the major that the more they approached the actual scene of conflagration the heat and smoke became less, until he saw that the fire was retreating before them and the following wind. In a few moments their haven of safety— the expanse already burnt over—came in sight. Here and there, seen dimly through the drifting smoke, the scattered embers that still strewed the forest floor glowed in weird nebulous spots like will-o'-the-wisps. For an instant the major hesitated; the sheriff cast a significant glance behind them.

"Go on; it's our only chance," he said imperatively.

They darted on, skimming the blackened or smouldering surface, which at times struck out sparks and flame from their heavier footprints as they passed. Their boots crackled and scorched beneath them; their shreds of clothing were on fire; their breathing became more difficult, until, providentially, they fell upon an abrupt, fissure-like depression of the soil, which the fire had leaped, and into which they blindly plunged and rolled together. A moment of relief and coolness followed, as they crept along the fissure, filled with damp and rotting leaves.

"Why not stay here?" said the exhausted prisoner.

"And be roasted like sweet potatoes when these trees catch," returned the sheriff grimly. "No." Even as he spoke, a dropping rain of fire spattered through the leaves from a splintered redwood, before overlooked, that was now blazing fiercely in the upper wind. A vague and indefinable terror was in the air. The conflagration no longer seemed to obey any rule of direction. The incendiary torch had passed invisibly everywhere. They scrambled out of the hollow, and again dashed desperately forward.

Beaten, bruised, blackened, and smoke-grimed—looking less human than the animals who had long since deserted the crest—they at last limped into a "wind opening" in the woods that the fire had skirted. The major sank exhaustedly to the ground; the sheriff threw himself beside him. Their strange relations to each other seemed to have been forgotten; they looked and acted as if they no longer thought of anything beyond the present. And when the sheriff finally arose and, disappearing for several minutes, brought his hat full of water for his prisoner from a distant spring that they had passed in their flight, he found him where he had left him—unchanged and unmoved.

He took the water gratefully, and after a pause fixed his eyes earnestly upon his captor. "I want you to do a favor to me," he said slowly. "I'm not going to offer you a bribe to do it either, nor ask you anything that isn't in a line with your duty. I think I understand you now, if I didn't before. Do you know Briggs's restaurant in Sacramento?"

The sheriff nodded.

"Well! over the restaurant are my private rooms, the finest in Sacramento. Nobody knows it but Briggs, and he has never told. They've been locked ever since I left; I've got the key still in my pocket. Now when we get to Sacramento, instead of taking me straight to jail, I want you to hold me THERE as your prisoner for a day and a night. I don't want to get away; you can take what precautions you like—surround the house with policemen, and sleep yourself in the ante-room. I don't want to destroy any papers or evidence; you can go through the rooms and examine everything before and after; I only want to stay there a day and a night; I want to be in my old rooms, have my meals from the restaurant as I used to, and sleep in my own bed once more. I want to live for one day like a gentleman, as I used to live before I came here. That's all! It isn't much, Tom. You can do it and say you require to do it to get evidence against me, or that you want to search the rooms."

The expression of wonder which had come into the sheriff's face at the beginning of this speech deepened into his old look of surly dissatisfaction. "And that's all ye want?" he said gloomily. "Ye don't want no friends—no lawyer? For I tell you, straight out, major, there ain't no hope for ye, when the law once gets hold of ye in Sacramento."

"That's all. Will you do it?"

The sheriff's face grew still darker. After a pause he said: "I don't say 'no,' and I don't say 'yes.' But," he added grimly, "it strikes me we'd better wait till we get clear o' these woods afore you think o' your Sacramento lodgings."

The major did not reply. The day had worn on, but the fire, now completely encircling them, opposed any passage in or out of that fateful barrier. The smoke of the burning underbrush hung low around them in a bank equally impenetrable to vision. They were as alone as shipwrecked sailors on an island, girded by a horizon of clouds.

"I'm going to try to sleep," said the major; "if your men

come you can waken me."

"And if YOUR men come?" said the sheriff dryly.

"Shoot me."

He lay down, closed his eyes, and to the sheriff's astonishment presently fell asleep. The sheriff, with his chin in his grimy hands, sat and watched him as the day slowly darkened around them and the distant fires came out in more lurid intensity. The face of the captive and outlawed murderer was singularly peaceful; that of the captor and man of duty was haggard, wild, and perplexed.

But even this changed soon. The sleeping man stirred restlessly and uneasily; his face began to work, his lips to move. "Tom," he gasped suddenly, "Tom!"

The sheriff bent over him eagerly. The sleeping man's eyes were still closed; beads of sweat stood upon his forehead. He was dreaming.

"Tom," he whispered, "take me out of this place—take me out from these dogs and pimps and beggars! Listen, Tom!—they're Sydney ducks, ticket-of-leave men, short card sharps, and sneak thieves! There isn't a gentleman among 'em! There isn't one I don't loathe and hate—and would grind under my heel, elsewhere. I'm a gentleman, Tom—yes, by God—an officer and a gentleman! I've served my country in the 9th Cavalry. That cub of West Point knows it and despises me, seeing me here in such company. That sergeant knows it—I recommended him for his first stripes for all he taunts me,—d—n him!"

"Come, wake up!" said the sheriff harshly.

The prisoner did not heed him; the sheriff shook him roughly, so roughly that the major's waistcoat and shirt dragged open, disclosing his fine silk undershirt, delicately worked and embroidered with golden thread. At the sight of this abased and faded magnificence the sheriff's hand was stayed; his eye wandered over the sleeping form before him. Yes, the hair was dyed too; near the roots it was quite white and grizzled; the pomatum was coming off the pointed moustache and imperial; the face in the light was very haggard; the lines from the angles of the nostril and mouth were like deep, half-healed gashes. The major was, without doubt, prematurely worn and played out.

The sheriff's persistent eyes, however, seemed to effect what his ruder hand could not. The sleeping man stirred, awoke to full consciousness, and sat up.

"Are they here? I'm ready," he said calmly.

"No," said the sheriff deliberately; "I only woke ye to say that I've been thinkin' over what ye asked me, and if we get to Sacramento all right, why, I'll do it and give ye that day and night at your old lodgings."

"Thank you."

The major reached out his hand; the sheriff hesitated, and then extended his own. The hands of the two men clasped for the first, and it would seem, the last time.

For the "cub of West Point" was, like most cubs, irritable when thwarted. And having been balked of his prey, the deserter, and possibly chaffed by his comrades for his profitless invasion of Wynyard's Bar, he had persuaded his commanding officer to give him permission to effect a recapture. Thus it came about that at dawn, filing along the ridge, on the outskirts of the fire, his heart was gladdened by the sight of the half-breed—with his hanging haversack belt and tattered army tunic— evidently still a fugitive, not a hundred yards away on the other side of the belt of fire, running down the hill with another ragged figure at his side. The command to "halt" was enforced by a single rifle shot over the fugitives' heads—but they still kept on their flight. Then the boy-officer snatched a carbine from one of his men, a volley rang out from the little troop—the shots of the privates mercifully high, those of the officer and sergeant leveled with wounded pride and full of deliberate purpose. The half-breed fell; so did his companion, and, rolling over together, both lay still.

But between the hunters and their fallen quarry reared a cheval de frise of flame and fallen timber impossible to cross. The young officer hesitated, shrugged his shoulders, wheeled his men about, and left the fire to correct any irregularity in his action.

It did not, however, change contemporaneous history, for a week later, when Wynyard's Bar discovered Major Overstone lying beside the man now recognized by them as the disguised sheriff of Siskyou, they rejoiced at this unfailing evidence of their lost leader's unequaled prowess. That he had again killed a sheriff and fought a whole posse, yielding only with his life, was never once doubted, and kept his memory green in Sierran chronicles long after Wynyard's Bar had itself become a memory.

A ROSE OF GLENBOGIE

The American consul at St. Kentigern stepped gloomily from the train at Whistlecrankie station. For the last twenty minutes his spirits had been slowly sinking before the drifting procession past the carriage windows of dull gray and brown hills—mammiform in shape, but so cold and sterile in expression that the swathes of yellow mist which lay in their hollows, like soiled guipure, seemed a gratuitous affectation of modesty. And when the train moved away, mingling its escaping steam with the slower mists of the mountain, he found himself alone on the platform—the only passenger and apparently the sole occupant of the station. He was gazing disconsolately at his trunk, which had taken upon itself a human loneliness in the emptiness of the place, when a railway porter stepped out of the solitary signal-box, where he had evidently been performing a double function, and lounged with exasperating deliberation towards him. He was a hard-featured man, with a thin fringe of yellow-gray whiskers that met under his chin like dirty strings to tie his cap on with.

"Ye'll be goin' to Glenbogie House, I'm thinkin'?" he said moodily.

The consul said that he was.

"I kenned it. Ye'll no be gettin' any machine to tak' ye there. They'll be sending a carriage for ye—if ye're EXPECTED." He glanced half doubtfully at the consul as if he was not quite so sure of it.

But the consul believed he WAS expected, and felt relieved at the certain prospect of a conveyance. The porter meanwhile surveyed him moodily.

"Ye'll be seein' Mistress MacSpadden there!"

The consul was surprised into a little over-consciousness. Mrs. MacSpadden was a vivacious acquaintance at St. Kentigern, whom he certainly—and not without some satisfaction—expected to meet at Glenbogie House. He raised his eyes inquiringly to the porter's.

"Ye'll no be rememberin' me. I had a machine in St. Kentigern and drove ye to MacSpadden's ferry often. Far, far too often! She's a strange flagrantitious creature; her husband's but a puir fule, I'm thinkin', and ye did yersel' nae guid gaunin' there."

It was a besetting weakness of the consul's that his sense of the ludicrous was too often reached before his more serious perceptions. The absurd combination of the bleak, inhospitable desolation before him, and the sepulchral complacency of his self-elected monitor, quite upset his gravity.

"Ay, ye'll be laughin' THE NOO," returned the porter with gloomy significance.

The consul wiped his eyes. "Still," he said demurely, "I trust you won't object to my giving you sixpence to carry my box to the carriage when it comes, and let the morality of this transaction devolve entirely upon me. Unless," he continued, even more gravely, as a spick and span brougham, drawn by two thoroughbreds, dashed out of the mist up to the platform, "unless you prefer to state the case to those two gentlemen"—pointing to the smart coachman and footman on the box—"and take THEIR opinion as to the propriety of my proceeding any further. It seems to me that their consciences ought to be consulted as well as yours. I'm only a stranger here, and am willing to do anything to conform to the local custom."

"It's a saxpence ye'll be payin' anyway," said the porter, grimly shouldering the trunk, "but I'll be no takin' any other mon's opinion on matters of my am dooty and conscience."

"Ah," said the consul gravely, "then you'll perhaps be allowing ME the same privilege."

The porter's face relaxed, and a gleam of approval—purely intellectual, however,—came into his eyes.

"Ye were always a smooth deevel wi' your tongue, Mr. Consul," he said, shouldering the box and walking off to the carriage.

Nevertheless, as soon as he was fairly seated and rattling away from the station, the consul had a flashing conviction that he had not only been grievously insulted but also that he had allowed the wife of an acquaintance to be spoken of disrespectfully in his presence. And he had done nothing! Yes—it was like him!—he had LAUGHED at the absurdity of the impertinence without resenting it! Another man would have slapped the porter's face! For an instant he hung out of the carriage window, intent upon ordering the coachman to drive back to the station, but the reflection—again a ludicrous one—that he would now be only bringing witnesses to a scene which might provoke a scandal more invidious to his acquaintance, checked him in time. But his spirits, momentarily diverted by the porter's effrontery, sunk to a lower ebb than before.

The clattering of his horses' hoofs echoed back from the rocky walls that occasionally hemmed in the road was not enlivening, but was less depressing than the recurring monotony of the open. The scenery did not suggest wildness to his alien eyes so much as it affected him with a vague sense of scorbutic impoverishment. It was not the loneliness of unfrequented nature, for there was a well-kept carriage road traversing its dreariness; and even when the hillside was clothed with scanty verdure, there were "outcrops" of smooth glistening weather-worn rocks showing like bare brown knees under the all too imperfectly kilted slopes. And at a little distance, lifting above a black drift of firs, were the square rigid sky lines of Glenbogie House, standing starkly against the cold, lingering northern twilight. As the vehicle turned, and rolled between two square stone gate-posts, the long avenue before him, though as well kept as the road, was but a slight improvement upon the outer sterility, and the dark iron-gray rectangular mansion beyond, guiltless of external decoration, even to the outlines of its small lustreless windows, opposed the grim inhospitable prospect with an equally grim inhospitable front. There were a few moments more of rapid driving, a swift swishing over soft gravel, the opening of a heavy door into a narrow vestibule, and then—a sudden sense of exquisitely diffused light and warmth from an arched and galleried central hall, the sounds of light laughter and subdued voices half lost in the airy space between the lofty pictured walls; the luxury of color in trophies, armor, and hangings; one or two careless groups before the recessed hearth or at the centre table, and the halted figure of a pretty woman on the broad, slow staircase. The contrast was sharp, ironical, and bewildering.

So much so that the consul, when he had followed the servant to his room, was impelled to draw aside the heavy window-curtains and look out again upon the bleak prospect it had half obliterated. The wing in which he was placed overhung a dark ravine or gully choked with shrubs and brambles that grew in a new luxuriance. As he gazed a large black bird floated upwards slowly from its depths, circled around the house with a few quick strokes of its wing, and then sped away—a black bolt—in one straight undeviating line towards the paling north. He still gazed into the abyss—half expecting another, even fancying he heard the occasional stir and flutter of obscure life below, and the melancholy call of nightfowl. A long-forgotten fragment of old English verse began to haunt him—

Hark! the raven flaps hys wing
In the briered dell belowe,
Hark! the dethe owl loude doth synge
To the night maers as thaie goe.

"Now, what put that stuff in my head?" he said as he turned impatiently from the window. "And why does this house, with all its interior luxury, hypocritically oppose such a forbidding front to its neighbors?" Then it occurred to him that perhaps the architect instinctively felt that a more opulent and elaborate exterior would only bring the poverty of surrounding nature into greater relief. But he was not in the habit of troubling himself with abstruse problems. A nearer recollection of the pretty frock he had seen on the staircase—in whose wearer he had just recognized his vivacious friend—turned his thoughts to her. He remembered how at their first meeting he had been interested in her bright audacity, unconventionality, and high spirits, which did not, however, amuse him as greatly as his later suspicion that she was playing a self-elected role, often with difficulty, opposition, and feverishness, rather than spontaneity. He remembered how he had watched her in the obtrusive assumption of a new fashion, in some reckless departure from an old one, or in some ostentatious disregard of certain hard and set rules of St. Kentigern; but that it never seemed to him that she was the happier for it. He even fancied that her mirth at such times had an undue nervousness; that her pluck—which was undoubted—had something of the defiance of despair, and that her persistence often had the grimness of duty rather than the thoughtlessness of pure amusement. What was she trying to do?—what was she trying to UNDO or forget? Her married life was apparently happy and even congenial. Her young husband was clever, complaisant, yet honestly devoted to her, even to the extension of a certain camaraderie to her admirers and a chivalrous protection by half-participation in her maddest freaks. Nor could he honestly say that her attitude towards his own sex—although marked by a freedom that often reached the verge of indiscretion—conveyed the least suggestion of passion or sentiment. The consul, more perceptive than analytical, found her a puzzle—who was, perhaps, the least mystifying to others who were content to sum up her eccentricities under the single vague epithet, "fast." Most women disliked her: she had a few associates among them, but no confidante, and even these were so unlike her, again, as to puzzle him still more. And yet he believed himself strictly impartial.

He walked to the window again, and looked down upon

the ravine from which the darkness now seemed to be slowly welling up and obliterating the landscape, and then, taking a book from his valise, settled himself in the easy-chair by the fire. He was in no hurry to join the party below, whom he had duly recognized and greeted as he passed through. They or their prototypes were familiar friends. There was the recently created baronet, whose "bloody hand" had apparently wiped out the stains of his earlier Radicalism, and whose former provincial self-righteousness had been supplanted by an equally provincial skepticism; there was his wife, who through all the difficulties of her changed position had kept the stalwart virtues of the Scotch bourgeoisie, and was— "decent"; there were the two native lairds that reminded him of "parts of speech," one being distinctly alluded to as a definite article, and the other being "of" something, and apparently governed always by that possessive case. There were two or three "workers"—men of power and ability in their several vocations; indeed, there was the general over-proportion of intellect, characteristic of such Scotch gatherings, and often in excess of minor social qualities. There was the usual foreigner, with Latin quickness, eagerness, and misapprehending adaptability. And there was the solitary Englishman—perhaps less generously equipped than the others—whom everybody differed from, ridiculed, and then looked up to and imitated. There were the half-dozen smartly frocked women, who, far from being the females of the foregoing species, were quite indistinctive, with the single exception of an American wife, who was infinitely more Scotch than her Scotch husband.

Suddenly he became aware of a faint rustling at his door, and what seemed to be a slight tap on the panel. He rose and opened it—the long passage was dark and apparently empty, but he fancied he could detect the quick swish of a skirt in the distance. As he re-entered his room, his eye fell for the first time on a rose whose stalk was thrust through the keyhole of his door. The consul smiled at this amiable solution of a mystery. It was undoubtedly the playful mischievousness of the vivacious MacSpadden. He placed it in water—intending to wear it in his coat at dinner as a gentle recognition of the fair donor's courtesy.

Night had thickened suddenly as from a passing cloud. He lit the two candles on his dressing-table, gave a glance into the now scarcely distinguishable abyss below his window, as he drew the curtains, and by the more diffused light for the first time surveyed his room critically. It was a larger apartment than that usually set aside for bachelors; the heavy four-poster had a conjugal reserve about it, and a tall cheval glass and certain minor details of the furniture suggested that it had been used for a married couple. He knew that the guest-rooms in country houses, as in hotels, carried no suggestion or flavor of the last tenant, and therefore lacked color and originality, and he was consequently surprised to find himself impressed with some distinctly novel atmosphere. He was puzzling himself to discover what it might be, when he again became aware of cautious footsteps apparently halting outside his door. This time he was prepared. With a half smile he stepped softly to the door and opened it suddenly. To his intense surprise he was face to face with a man.

But his discomfiture was as nothing compared to that of the stranger—whom he at once recognized as one of his fellow-guests—the youthful Laird of Whistlecrankie. The young fellow's healthy color at once paled, then flushed a deep crimson, and a forced smile stiffened his mouth.

"I—beg your par-r-rdon," he said with a nervous

brusqueness that brought out his accent. "I couldna find ma room. It'll be changed, and I—"

"Perhaps I have got it," interrupted the consul smilingly. "I've only just come, and they've put me in here."

"Nae! Nae!" said the young man hurriedly, "it's no' thiss. That is, it's no' mine noo."

"Won't you come in?" suggested the consul politely, holding open the door.

The young man entered the room with the quick strides but the mechanical purposelessness of embarrassment. Then he stiffened and stood erect. Yet in spite of all this he was strikingly picturesque and unconventional in his Highland dress, worn with the freedom of long custom and a certain lithe, barbaric grace. As the consul continued to gaze at him encouragingly, the quick resentful pride of a shy man suddenly mantled his high cheekbones, and with an abrupt "I'll not deesturb ye longer," he strode out of the room.

The consul watched the easy swing of his figure down the passage, and then closed the door. "Delightful creature," he said musingly, "and not so very unlike an Apache chief either! But what was he doing outside my door? And was it HE who left that rose—not as a delicate Highland attention to an utter stranger, but"—the consul's mouth suddenly expanded—"to some fair previous occupant? Or was it really HIS room—he looked as if he were lying— and"—here the consul's mouth expanded even more wickedly—"and Mrs. MacSpadden had put the flower there for him." This implied snub to his vanity was, however, more than compensated by his wicked antici- pation of the pretty perplexity of his fair friend when HE should appear at dinner with the flower in his own buttonhole. It would serve her right, the arrant flirt! But here he was interrupted by the entrance of a tall housemaid with his hot water.

"I am afraid I've dispossessed Mr.—Mr.—Kilcraithie rather prematurely," said the consul lightly.

To his infinite surprise the girl answered with grim decision, "Nane too soon."

The consul stared. "I mean," he explained, "that I found him hesitating here in the passage, looking for his room."

"Ay, he's always hoaverin' and glowerin' in the passages —but it's no' for his ROOM! And it's a deesgrace to decent Christian folk his carryin' on wi' married weemen —mebbee they're nae better than he!"

"That will do," said the consul curtly. He had no desire to encourage a repetition of the railway porter's freedom.

"Ye'll no fash yoursel' aboot HIM," continued the girl, without heeding the rebuff. "It's no' the meestreess' wish that he's keepit here in the wing reserved for married folk, and she's no' sorry for the excuse to pit ye in his place. Ye'll be married yoursel', I'm hearin'. But, I ken ye's nae mair to be lippened tae for THAT."

This was too much for the consul's gravity. "I'm afraid," he said with diplomatic gayety, "that although I am married, as I haven't my wife with me, I've no right to this superior accommodation and comfort. But you can assure your mistress that I'll try to deserve them."

"Ay," said the girl, but with no great confidence in her

voice as she grimly quitted the room.

"When our foot's upon our native heath, whether our name's Macgregor or Kilcraithie, it would seem that we must tread warily," mused the consul as he began to dress. "But I'm glad she didn't see that rose, or MY reputation would have been ruined." Here another knock at the door arrested him. He opened it impatiently to a tall gillie, who instantly strode into the room. There was such another suggestion of Kilcraithie in the man and his manner that the consul instantly divined that he was Kilcraithie's servant.

"I'll be takin' some bit things that yon Whistlecrankie left," said the gillie gravely, with a stolid glance around the room.

"Certainly," said the consul; "help yourself." He continued his dressing as the man began to rummage in the empty drawers. The consul had his back towards him, but, looking in the glass of the dressing-table, he saw that the gillie was stealthily watching him. Suddenly he passed before the mantelpiece and quickly slipped the rose from its glass into his hand.

"I'll trouble you to put that back," said the consul quietly, without turning round. The gillie slid a quick glance towards the door, but the consul was before him. "I don't think THAT was left by your master," he said in an ostentatiously calm voice, for he was conscious of an absurd and inexplicable tumult in his blood, "and perhaps you'd better put it back."

The man looked at the flower with an attention that might have been merely ostentatious, and replaced it in the glass.

Bret Harte

"A thocht it was hiss."

"And I think it isn't," said the consul, opening the door.

Yet when the man had passed out he was by no means certain that the flower was not Kilcraithie's. He was even conscious that if the young Laird had approached him with a reasonable explanation or appeal he would have yielded it up. Yet here he was—looking angrily pale in the glass, his eyes darker than they should be, and with an unmistakable instinct to do battle for this idiotic gage! Was there some morbid disturbance in the air that was affecting him as it had Kilcraithie? He tried to laugh, but catching sight of its sardonic reflection in the glass became grave again. He wondered if the gillie had been really looking for anything his master had left—he had certainly TAKEN nothing. He opened one or two of the drawers, and found only a woman's tortoiseshell hairpin—overlooked by the footman when he had emptied them for the consul's clothes. It had been probably forgotten by some fair and previous tenant to Kilcraithie. The consul looked at his watch—it was time to go down. He grimly pinned the fateful flower in his buttonhole, and half-defiantly descended to the drawing-room.

Here, however, he was inclined to relax when, from a group of pretty women, the bright gray eyes of Mrs. MacSpadden caught his, were suddenly diverted to the lapel of his coat, and then leaped up to his again with a sparkle of mischief. But the guests were already pairing off in dinner couples, and as they passed out of the room, he saw that she was on the arm of Kilcraithie. Yet, as she passed him, she audaciously turned her head, and in a mischievous affectation of jealous reproach, murmured:—

"So soon!"

At dinner she was too far removed for any conversation with him, although from his seat by his hostess he could plainly see her saucy profile midway up the table. But, to his surprise, her companion, Kilcraithie, did not seem to be responding to her gayety. By turns abstracted and feverish, his glances occasionally wandered towards the end of the table where the consul was sitting. For a few moments he believed that the affair of the flower, combined, perhaps, with the overhearing of Mrs. MacSpadden's mischievous sentence, rankled in the Laird's barbaric soul. But he became presently aware that Kilcraithie's eyes eventually rested upon a quiet-looking blonde near the hostess. Yet the lady not only did not seem to be aware of it, but her face was more often turned towards the consul, and their eyes had once or twice met. He had been struck by the fact that they were half-veiled but singularly unimpassioned eyes, with a certain expression of cold wonderment and criticism quite inconsistent with their veiling. Nor was he surprised when, after a preliminary whispering over the plates, his hostess presented him. The lady was the young wife of the middle-aged dignitary who, seated further down the table, opposite Mrs. MacSpadden, was apparently enjoying that lady's wildest levities. The consul bowed, the lady leaned a little forward.

"We were saying what a lovely rose you had."

The consul's inward response was "Hang that flower!" His outward expression was the modest query:—

"Is it SO peculiar?"

"No; but it's very pretty. Would you allow me to see it?"

Disengaging the flower from his buttonhole he handed it

to her. Oddly enough, it seemed to him that half the table was watching and listening to them. Suddenly the lady uttered a little cry. "Dear me! it's full of thorns; of course you picked and arranged it yourself, for any lady would have wrapped something around the stalk!"

But here there was a burlesque outcry and a good-humored protest from the gentlemen around her against this manifestly leading question. "It's no fair! Ye'll not answer her—for the dignity of our sex." Yet in the midst of it, it suddenly occurred to the consul that there HAD been a slip of paper wrapped around it, which had come off and remained in the keyhole. The blue eyes of the lady were meanwhile sounding his, but he only smiled and said:—

"Then it seems it IS peculiar?"

When the conversation became more general he had time to observe other features of the lady than her placid eyes. Her light hair was very long, and grew low down the base of her neck. Her mouth was firm, the upper lip slightly compressed in a thin red line, but the lower one, although equally precise at the corners, became fuller in the centre and turned over like a scarlet leaf, or, as it struck him suddenly, like the tell-tale drop of blood on the mouth of a vampire. Yet she was very composed, practical, and decorous, and as the talk grew more animated—and in the vicinity of Mrs. MacSpadden, more audacious—she kept a smiling reserve of expression,—which did not, however, prevent her from following that lively lady, whom she evidently knew, with a kind of encouraging attention.

"Kate is in full fling to-night," she said to the hostess. Lady Macquoich smiled ambiguously—so ambiguously that the consul thought it necessary to interfere for his friend. "She seems to say what most of us think, but I am afraid very few of us could voice as innocently," he smilingly suggested.

"She is a great friend of yours," returned the lady, looking at him through her half-veiled lids. "She has made us quite envy her."

"And I am afraid made it impossible for ME to either sufficiently thank her or justify her taste," he said quietly. Yet he was vexed at an unaccountable resentment which had taken possession of him—who but a few hours before had only laughed at the porter's criticism.

After the ladies had risen, the consul with an instinct of sympathy was moving up towards "Jock" MacSpadden, who sat nearer the host, when he was stopped midway of the table by the dignitary who had sat opposite to Mrs. MacSpadden. "Your frien' is maist amusing wi' her audacious tongue—ay, and her audacious ways," he said with large official patronage; "and we've enjoyed her here immensely, but I hae mae doots if mae Leddy Macquoich taks as kindly to them. You and I—men of the wurrld, I may say—we understand them for a' their worth; ay!—ma wife too, with whom I observed ye speakin'—is maist tolerant of her, but man! it's extraordinar'"—he lowered his voice slightly—"that yon husband of hers does na' check her freedoms with Kilcraithie. I wadna' say anythin' was wrong, ye ken, but is he no' over confident and conceited aboot his wife?"

"I see you don't know him," said the consul smilingly, "and I'd be delighted to make you acquainted. Jock," he continued, raising his voice as he turned towards MacSpadden, "let me introduce you to Sir Alan Deeside, who don't know YOU, although he's a great admirer of your wife;" and unheeding the embarrassed protestations of Sir Alan and the laughing assertions of Jock that they were already acquainted, he moved on beside his host. That hospitable knight, who had been airing his knowledge of London smart society to his English guest with a singular mixture of assertion and obsequiousness, here stopped short. "Ay, sit down, laddie, it was so guid of ye to come, but I'm thinkin' at your end of the table ye lost the bit fun of Mistress MacSpadden. Eh, but she was unco' lively to-night. 'Twas all Kilcraithie could do to keep her from proposin' your health with Hieland honors, and offerin' to lead off with her ain foot on the table! Ay, and she'd ha' done it. And that's a braw rose she's been givin' ye—and ye got out of it claverly wi' Lady Deeside."

When he left the table with the others to join the ladies, the same unaccountable feeling of mingled shyness and nervous irascibility still kept possession of him. He felt that in his present mood he could not listen to any further criticisms of his friend without betraying some unwonted heat, and as his companions filed into the drawing-room he slipped aside in the hope of recovering his equanimity by a few moments' reflection in his own room. He glided quickly up the staircase and entered the corridor. The passage that led to his apartment was quite dark, especially before his door, which was in a bay that really ended the passage. He was consequently surprised and somewhat alarmed at seeing a shadowy female figure hovering before it. He instinctively halted; the figure became more distinct from some luminous halo that seemed to encompass it. It struck him that this was only the light of his fire thrown through his open door, and that the figure was probably that of a servant before it, who had been arranging his room. He started forward again, but at the sound of his advancing footsteps the figure and the luminous glow vanished, and he arrived blankly face to face with his own closed door. He looked around the dim bay; it was absolutely vacant. It was equally impossible for any one to have escaped without passing him. There was only his room left. A half-nervous, half-superstitious thrill crept over him as he suddenly grasped the handle of the door and threw it open. The leaping light of his fire revealed its emptiness: no one was there! He lit the candle and peered behind the curtains and furniture and under the bed; the room was as vacant and undisturbed as when he left it.

Had it been a trick of his senses or a bona-fide apparition? He had never heard of a ghost at Glenbogie—the house dated back some fifty years; Sir John Macquoich's tardy knighthood carried no such impedimenta. He looked down wonderingly on the flower in his buttonhole. Was there something uncanny in that innocent blossom? But here he was struck by another recollection, and examined the keyhole of his door. With the aid of the tortoiseshell hairpin he dislodged the paper he had forgotten. It was only a thin spiral strip, apparently the white outer edge of some newspaper, and it certainly seemed to be of little service as a protection against the thorns of the rose-stalk. He was holding it over the fire, about to drop it into the blaze, when the flame revealed some pencil-marks upon it. Taking it to the candle he read, deeply bitten into the paper by a hard pencil-point: "At half-past one." There was nothing else—no signature; but the handwriting was NOT Mrs. MacSpadden's!

Then whose? Was it that of the mysterious figure whom he had just seen? Had he been selected as the medium of some spiritual communication, and, perhaps, a ghostly visitation later on? Or was he the victim of some clever trick? He had once witnessed such dubious attempts to relieve the monotony of a country house. He again examined the room carefully, but without avail. Well! the mystery or trick would be revealed at half-past one. It was a somewhat inconvenient hour, certainly. He looked down at the baleful gift in his buttonhole, and for a moment felt inclined to toss it in the fire. But this was quickly followed by his former revulsion of resentment and defiance. No! he would wear it, no matter what happened, until its material or spiritual owner came for it. He closed the door and returned to the drawing-room.

Midway of the staircase he heard the droning of pipes. There was dancing in the drawing-room to the music of the gorgeous piper who had marshaled them to dinner. He was not sorry, as he had no inclination to talk, and the one confidence he had anticipated with Mrs. MacSpadden was out of the question now. He had no right to reveal his later discovery. He lingered a few moments in the hall. The buzzing of the piper's drones gave him that impression of confused and blindly aggressive intoxication which he had often before noticed in this barbaric instrument, and had always seemed to him as the origin of its martial inspiration. From this he was startled by voices and steps in the gallery he had just quitted, but which came from the opposite direction to his room. It was Kilcraithie and Mrs. MacSpadden. As she caught sight of him, he fancied she turned slightly and aggressively pale, with a certain hardening of her mischievous eyes. Nevertheless, she descended the staircase more deliberately than her companion, who brushed past him with an embarrassed self-consciousness, quite in advance of her. She lingered for an instant.

"You are not dancing?" she said.

"No."

"Perhaps you are more agreeably employed?"

"At this exact moment, certainly."

She cast a disdainful glance at him, crossed the hall, and followed Kilcraithie.

"Hang me, if I understand it all!" mused the consul, by no means good-humoredly. "Does she think I have been spying upon her and her noble chieftain? But it's just as well that I didn't tell her anything."

He turned to follow them. In the vestibule he came upon a figure which had halted before a large pier-glass. He recognized M. Delfosse, the French visitor, complacently twisting the peak of his Henri Quatre beard. He would have passed without speaking, but the Frenchman glanced smilingly at the consul and his buttonhole. Again the flower!

"Monsieur is decore," he said gallantly.

The consul assented, but added, not so gallantly, that though they were not in France he might still be unworthy of it. The baleful flower had not improved his temper. Nor did the fact that, as he entered the room, he thought the people stared at him—until he saw that their attention was directed to Lady Deeside, who had entered almost behind him. From his hostess, who had offered him a seat beside her, he gathered that M. Delfosse and Kilcraithie had each temporarily occupied his room, but that they had been transferred to the other wing, apart from the married couples and young ladies, because when they came upstairs from the billiard and card room late, they sometimes disturbed the fair occupants. No!—there were no ghosts at Glenbogie. Mysterious footsteps had sometimes been heard in the ladies' corridor, but—with peculiar significance—she was AFRAID they could be easily accounted for. Sir Alan, whose room was next to the MacSpaddens', had been disturbed by them.

He was glad when it was time to escape to the billiard-room and tobacco. For a while he forgot the evening's adventure, but eventually found himself listening to a discussion—carried on over steaming tumblers of toddy—in regard to certain predispositions of the always debatable sex.

"Ye'll not always judge by appearances," said Sir Alan. "Ye'll mind the story o' the meenester's wife of Aiblinnoch. It was thocht that she was ower free wi' one o' the parishioners—ay! it was the claish o' the whole kirk, while none dare tell the meenester hisself—bein' a bookish, simple, unsuspectin' creeter. At last one o' the elders bethocht him of a bit plan of bringing it home to the wife, through the gospel lips of her ain husband! So he intimated to the meenester his suspicions of grievous laxity amang the female flock, and of the necessity of a special sermon on the Seventh Command. The puir man consented—although he dinna ken why and wherefore—and preached a gran' sermon! Ay, man! it was crammed wi' denunciation and an emptyin' o' the vials o' wrath! The congregation sat dumb as huddled sheep—when they were no' starin' and gowpin' at the meenester's wife settin' bolt upright in her place. And then, when the air was blue wi' sulphur frae tae pit, the meenester's wife up rises! Man! Ivry eye was spearin' her—ivry lug was prickt towards her! And she goes out in the aisle facin' the meenester, and—"

Sir Alan paused.

"And what?" demanded the eager auditory.

"She pickit up the elder's wife, sobbin' and tearin' her hair in strong hysterics."

At the end of a relieved pause Sir Alan slowly concluded: "It was said that the elder removed frae Aiblinnoch wi' his wife, but no' till he had effected a change of meenesters."

It was already past midnight, and the party had dropped off one by one, with the exception of Deeside, Macquoich, the young Englishman, and a Scotch laird, who were playing poker—an amusement which he understood they frequently protracted until three in the morning. It was nearly time for him to expect his mysterious visitant. Before he went upstairs he thought he would take a breath of the outer evening air, and throwing a mackintosh over his shoulders, passed out of the garden door of the billiard-room. To his surprise it gave immediately upon the fringe of laurel that hung over the chasm.

It was quite dark; the few far-spread stars gave scarcely any light, and the slight auroral glow towards the north was all that outlined the fringe of the abyss, which might have proved dangerous to any unfamiliar wanderer. A damp breath of sodden leaves came from its depths. Beside him stretched the long dark facade of the wing he inhabited, his own window the only one that showed a faint light. A few paces beyond, a singular structure of rustic wood and glass, combining the peculiarities of a sentry-box, a summer-house, and a shelter, was built against the blank wall of the wing. He imagined the monotonous prospect from its windows of the tufted chasm, the coldly profiled northern hills beyond,—and shivered. A little further on, sunk in the wall like a postern, was a small door that evidently gave easy egress to seekers of this stern retreat. In the still air a faint grating sound like the passage of a foot across gravel came to him as from the distance. He paused, thinking he had been followed by one of the card-players, but saw no one, and the sound was not repeated.

It was past one. He re-entered the billiard-room, passed the unchanged group of card-players, and taking a candlestick from the hall ascended the dark and silent staircase into the corridor. The light of his candle cast a flickering halo around him—but did not penetrate the gloomy distance. He at last halted before his door, gave a scrutinizing glance around the embayed recess, and opened the door half expectantly. But the room was empty as he had left it.

It was a quarter past one. He threw himself on the bed without undressing, and fixed his eyes alternately on the door and his watch. Perhaps the unwonted seriousness of his attitude struck him, but a sudden sense of the preposterousness of the whole situation, of his solemnly ridiculous acceptance of a series of mere coincidences as a foregone conclusion, overcame him, and he laughed. But in the same breath he stopped.

There WERE footsteps approaching—cautious foot-steps—but not at his door! They were IN THE ROOM—no! in the WALL just behind him! They were descending some staircase at the back of his bed—he could hear the regular tap of a light slipper from step to step and the rustle of a skirt seemingly in his very ear. They were becoming less and less distinct—they were gone! He sprang to his feet, but almost at the same instant he was conscious of a sudden chill—that seemed to him as physical as it was mental. The room was slowly suffused with a cool sodden breath and the dank odor of rotten leaves. He looked at the candle—its flame was actually deflecting in this mysterious blast. It seemed to come from a recess for hanging clothes topped by a heavy cornice and curtain. He had examined it before, but he drew the curtain once more aside. The cold current certainly seemed to be more perceptible there. He felt the red-clothed backing of the interior, and his hand suddenly grasped a doorknob. It turned, and the whole structure—cornice and curtains—swung inwards towards him with THE DOOR ON WHICH IT WAS HUNG! Behind it was a dark staircase leading from the floor above to some outer door below, whose opening had given ingress to the chill humid current from the ravine. This was the staircase where he had just heard the footsteps—and this was, no doubt, the door through which the mysterious figure had vanished from his room a few hours before!

Taking his candle, he cautiously ascended the stairs until he found himself on the landing of the suites of the married couples and directly opposite to the rooms of the MacSpaddens and Deesides. He was about to descend again when he heard a far-off shout, a scuffling sound on the outer gravel, and the frenzied shaking of the handle of the lower door. He had hardly time to blow out his candle and flatten himself against the wall, when the door was flung open and a woman frantically flew up the staircase. His own door was still open; from within its depths the light of his fire projected a flickering beam across the steps. As she rushed past it the light revealed her face; it needed not the peculiar perfume of her garments as she swept by his concealed figure to make him recognize—Lady Deeside!

Amazed and confounded, he was about to descend, when he heard the lower door again open. But here a sudden instinct bade him pause, turn, and reascend to the upper landing. There he calmly relit his candle, and made his way down to the corridor that overlooked the central hall. The sound of suppressed voices—speaking with the exhausted pauses that come from spent excitement—made him cautious again, and he halted. It was the card party slowly passing from the billiard-room to the hall.

"Ye owe it yoursel'—to your wife—not to pit up with it a day longer," said the subdued voice of Sir Alan. "Man! ye war in an ace o' havin' a braw scandal."

"Could ye no' get your wife to speak till her," responded Macquoich, "to gie her a hint that she's better awa' out of this? Lady Deeside has some influence wi' her."

The consul ostentatiously dropped the extinguisher from his candlestick. The party looked up quickly. Their faces were still flushed and agitated, but a new restraint seemed to come upon them on seeing him.

"I thought I heard a row outside," said the consul explanatorily.

They each looked at their host without speaking.

"Oh, ay," said Macquoich, with simulated heartiness, "a bit fuss between the Kilcraithie and yon Frenchman; but they're baith goin' in the mornin'."

"I thought I heard MacSpadden's voice," said the consul quietly.

There was a dead silence. Then Macquoich said hurriedly:—

"Is he no' in his room—in bed—asleep,—man?"

"I really don't know; I didn't inquire," said the consul with a slight yawn. "Good night!"

He turned, not without hearing them eagerly whispering again, and entered the passage leading to his own room. As he opened the door he was startled to find the subject of his inquiry—Jock MacSpadden—quietly seated in his armchair by his fire.

"Jock!"

"Don't be alarmed, old man; I came up by that staircase and saw the door open, and guessed you'd be returning soon. But it seemed you went ROUND BY THE CORRIDOR," he said, glancing curiously at the consul's face. "Did you meet the crowd?"

"Yes, Jock! WHAT does it all mean?"

MacSpadden laughed. "It means that I was just in time to keep Kilbraithie from chucking Delfosse down that ravine; but they both scooted when they saw me. By Jove! I don't know which was the most frightened."

"But," said the consul slowly, "what was it all about, Jock?"

"Some gallantry of that d—d Frenchman, who's trying to do some woman-stalking up here, and jealousy of Kilcraithie's, who's just got enough of his forbears' blood in him to think nothing of sticking three inches of his dirk in the wame of the man that crosses him. But I say," continued Jock, leaning easily back in his chair, "YOU ought to know something of all this. This room, old man, was used as a sort of rendezvous, having two outlets, don't you see, when they couldn't get at the summer-house below. By Jove! they both had it in turns—Kilcraithie and the Frenchman—until Lady Macquoich got wind of something, swept them out, and put YOU in it."

The consul rose and approached his friend with a grave face. "Jock, I DO know something about it—more about it than any one thinks. You and I are old friends. Shall I tell you WHAT I know?"

Jock's handsome face became a trifle paler, but his frank, clear eyes rested steadily on the consul's.

"Go on!" he said.

"I know that this flower which I am wearing was the signal for the rendezvous this evening," said the consul slowly, "and this paper," taking it from his pocket, "contained the time of the meeting, written in the lady's own hand. I know who she was, for I saw her face as plainly as I see yours now, by the light of the same fire; it was as pale, but not as frank as yours, old man. That is what I know. But I know also what people THINK they know, and for that reason I put that paper in YOUR hand. It is yours—your vindication—your REVENGE, if you choose. Do with it what you like."

Jock, with unchanged features and undimmed eyes, took the paper from the consul's hand, without looking at it.

"I may do with it what I like?" he repeated.

"Yes."

He was about to drop it into the fire, but the consul stayed his hand.

"Are you not going to LOOK at the handwriting first?"

There was a moment of silence. Jock raised his eyes with a sudden flash of pride in them and said, "No!"

The friends stood side by side, grasping each other's hands, as the burning paper leaped up the chimney in a vanishing flame.

"Do you think you have done quite right, Jock, in view of any scandal you may hear?"

"Quite! You see, old man, I know MY WIFE—but I don't think that Deeside KNOWS HIS."

THE MYSTERY OF THE HACIENDA

Dick Bracy gazed again at the Hacienda de los Osos, and hesitated. There it lay—its low whitewashed walls looking like a quartz outcrop of the long lazy hillside—unmistakably hot, treeless, and staring broadly in the uninterrupted Californian sunlight. Yet he knew that behind those blistering walls was a reposeful patio, surrounded by low-pitched verandas; that the casa was full of roomy corridors, nooks, and recesses, in which lurked the shadows of a century, and that hidden by the further wall was a lonely old garden, hoary with gnarled pear-trees, and smothered in the spice and dropping leaves of its baking roses. He knew that, although the unwinking sun might glitter on its red tiles, and the unresting trade winds whistle around its angles, it always kept one unvarying temperature and untroubled calm, as if the dignity of years had triumphed over the changes of ephemeral seasons. But would others see it with his eyes? Would his practical, housekeeping aunt, and his pretty modern cousin—

"Well, what do you say? Speak the word, and you can go into it with your folks to-morrow. And I reckon you won't want to take anything either, for you'll find everything there—just as the old Don left it. I don't want it; the land is good enough for me; I shall have my vaqueros and rancheros to look after the crops and the cattle, and they won't trouble you, for their sheds and barns will be two miles away. You can stay there as long as you like, and go when you choose. You might like to try it for a spell; it's all the same to me. But I should think it the sort of thing a man like you would fancy, and it seems the right thing to have you there. Well,—what shall it be? Is it a go?"

Dick knew that the speaker was sincere. It was an offer perfectly characteristic of his friend, the Western millionaire, who had halted by his side. And he knew also that the slow lifting of his bridle-rein, preparatory to starting forward again, was the business-like gesture of a man who wasted no time even over his acts of impulsive liberality. In another moment he would dismiss the unaccepted offer from his mind—without concern and without resentment.

"Thank you—it is a go," said Dick gratefully.

Nevertheless, when he reached his own little home in the outskirts of San Francisco that night, he was a trifle nervous in confiding to the lady, who was at once his aunt and housekeeper, the fact that he was now the possessor of a huge mansion in whose patio alone the little eight-roomed villa where they had lived contentedly might be casually dropped. "You see, Aunt Viney," he hurriedly explained, "it would have been so ungrateful to have refused him—and it really was an offer as spontaneous as it was liberal. And then, you see, we need occupy only a part of the casa."

"And who will look after the other part?" said Aunt Viney grimly. "That will have to be kept tidy, too; and the servants for such a house, where in heaven are they to come from? Or do they go with it?"

"No," said Dick quickly; "the servants left with their old master, when Ringstone bought the property. But we'll find servants enough in the neighborhood—Mexican peons and Indians, you know."

Aunt Viney sniffed. "And you'll have to entertain—if it's a big house. There are all your Spanish neighbors. They'll be gallivanting in and out all the time."

"They won't trouble us," he returned, with some hesitation. "You see, they're furious at the old Don for disposing of his lands to an American, and they won't be likely to look upon the strangers in the new place as anything but interlopers."

"Oh, that is it, is it?" ejaculated Aunt Viney, with a slight puckering of her lips. "I thought there was SOMETHING."

"My dear aunt," said Dick, with a sudden illogical heat which he tried to suppress; "I don't know what you mean by 'it' and 'something.' Ringstone's offer was perfectly unselfish; he certainly did not suppose that I would be affected, any more than he would he, by the childish sentimentality of these people over a legitimate, every-day business affair. The old Don made a good bargain, and simply sold the land he could no longer make profitable with his obsolete method of farming, his gang of idle retainers, and his Noah's Ark machinery, to a man who knew how to use steam reapers, and hired sensible men to work on shares." Nevertheless he was angry with himself for making any explanation, and still more disturbed that he was conscious of a certain feeling that it was necessary.

"I was thinking," said Aunt Viney quietly, "that if we

invited anybody to stay with us—like Cecily, for example —it might be rather dull for her if we had no neighbors to introduce her to."

Dick started; he had not thought of this. He had been greatly influenced by the belief that his pretty cousin, who was to make them a visit, would like the change and would not miss excitement. "We can always invite some girls down there and make our own company," he answered cheerfully. Nevertheless, he was dimly conscious that he had already made an airy castle of the old hacienda, in which Cecily and her aunt moved ALONE. It was to Cecily that he would introduce the old garden, it was Cecily whom he would accompany through the dark corridors, and with whom he would lounge under the awnings of the veranda. All this innocently, and without prejudice or ulterior thought. He was not yet in love with the pretty cousin whom he had seen but once or twice during the past few years, but it was a possibility not unpleasant to occasionally contemplate. Yet it was equally possible that she might yearn for lighter companionship and accustomed amusement; that the passion-fringed garden and shadow-haunted corridor might be profaned by hoydenish romping and laughter, or by that frivolous flirtation which, in others, he had always regarded as commonplace and vulgar.

Howbeit, at the end of two weeks he found himself regularly installed in the Hacienda de los Osos. His little household, re-enforced by his cousin Cecily and three peons picked up at Los Pinos, bore their transplantation with a singular equanimity that seemed to him unaccountable. Then occurred one of those revelations of character with which Nature is always ready to trip up merely human judgment. Aunt Viney, an unrelenting widow of calm but unshaken Dutch prejudices, high but narrow in religious belief, merged without a murmur into the position of chatelaine of this unconventional, half-Latin household. Accepting the situation without exaltation or criticism, placid but unresponsive amidst the youthful enthusiasm of Dick and Cecily over each quaint detail, her influence was, nevertheless, felt throughout the lingering length and shadowy breadth of the strange old house. The Indian and Mexican servants, at first awed by her practical superiority, succumbed to her half-humorous toleration of their incapacity, and became her devoted slaves. Dick was astonished, and even Cecily was confounded. "Do you know," she said confidentially to her cousin, "that when that brown Conchita thought to please Aunty by wearing white stockings instead of going round as usual with her cinnamon-colored bare feet in yellow slippers—which I was afraid would be enough to send Aunty into conniption fits—she actually told her, very quietly, to take them off, and dress according to her habits and her station? And you remember that in her big, square bedroom there is a praying-stool and a ghastly crucifix, at least three feet long, in ivory and black, quite too human for anything? Well, when I offered to put them in the corridor, she said I 'needn't trouble'; that really she hadn't noticed them, and they would do very well where they were. You'd think she had been accustomed to this sort of thing all her life. It's just too sweet of her, any way, even if she's shamming. And if she is, she just does it to the life too, and could give those Spanish women points. Why, she rode en pillion on Manuel's mule, behind him, holding on by his sash, across to the corral yesterday; and you should have seen Manuel absolutely scrape the ground before her with his sombrero when he let her down." Indeed, her tall, erect figure in black lustreless silk, appearing in a heavily shadowed doorway, or seated in a recessed window, gave a new and patrician dignity to the melancholy of the hacienda. It was pleasant to follow this quietly ceremonious shadow gliding along the rose garden at twilight, halting at times to bend stiffly over the bushes, garden-shears in hand, and carrying a little basket filled with withered but still odorous petals, as if she were grimly gathering the faded roses of her youth.

It was also probable that the lively Cecily's appreciation of her aunt might have been based upon another virtue of that lady—namely, her exquisite tact in dealing with the delicate situation evolved from the always possible relations of the two cousins. It was not to be supposed that the servants would fail to invest the young people with Southern romance, and even believe that the situation was prearranged by the aunt with a view to their eventual engagement. To deal with the problem openly, yet without startling the consciousness of either Dick or Cecily; to allow them the privileges of children subject to the occasional restraints of childhood; to find certain household duties for the young girl that kept them naturally apart until certain hours of general relaxation; to calmly ignore the meaning of her retainers' smiles and glances, and yet to good-humoredly accept their interest as a kind of feudal loyalty, was part of Aunt Viney's deep diplomacy. Cecily enjoyed her freedom and companion-ship with Dick, as she enjoyed the novel experiences of the old house, the quaint, faded civilization that it represented, and the change and diversion always acceptable to youth. She did not feel the absence of other girls of her own age; neither was she aware that through this omission she was spared the necessity of a confidante or a rival—both equally revealing to her thoughtless enjoyment. They took their rides together openly and without concealment, relating their adventures afterwards to Aunt Viney with a naivete and frankness that dreamed of no suppression. The city-bred Cecily, accustomed to horse exercise solely as an ornamental and artificial recreation, felt for the first time the fearful joy of a dash across a league-long plain, with no onlookers but the scattered wild horses she might startle up to scurry before her, or race at her side. Small wonder that, mounted on her fiery little mustang, untrammeled by her short gray riding-habit, free as the wind itself that blew through the folds of her flannel blouse, with her brown hair half-loosed beneath her slouched felt hat, she seemed to Dick a more beautiful and womanly figure than the stiff buckramed simulation of man's angularity and precision he had seen in the parks. Perhaps one day she detected this consciousness too plainly in his persistent eyes. Up to that moment she had only watched the glittering stretches of yellow grain, in which occasional wind-shorn ever-green oaks stood mid-leg deep like cattle in water, the distant silhouette of the Sierras against the steely blue, or perhaps the frankly happy face of the good-looking young fellow at her side. But it seemed to her now that an intruder had entered the field—a stranger before whom she was impelled to suddenly fly—half-laughingly, half-affrightedly—the anxious Dick following wonderingly at her mustang's heels, until she reached the gates of the hacienda, where she fell into a gravity and seriousness that made him wonder still more. He did not dream that his guileless cousin had discovered, with a woman's instinct, a mysterious invader who sought to share their guileless companionship, only to absorb it entirely, and that its name was—love!

The next day she was so greatly preoccupied with her household duties that she could not ride with him. Dick felt unaccountably lost. Perhaps this check to their daily intercourse was no less accelerating to his feelings than the vague motive that induced Cecily to withhold herself. He moped in the corridor; he rode out alone, bullying his mustang in proportion as he missed his cousin's gentle companionship, and circling aimlessly, but still unconsciously, around the hacienda as a centre of attraction. The sun at last was sinking to the accompaniment of a rising wind, which seemed to blow and scatter its broad rays over the shimmering plain until every slight protuberance was burnished into startling brightness; the shadows of the short green oaks grew disproportionally long, and all seemed to point to the white-walled casa. Suddenly he started and instantly reined up.

The figure of a young girl, which he had not before noticed, was slowly moving down the half-shadowed lane made by the two walls of the garden and the corral. Cecily! Perhaps she had come out to meet him. He spurred forward; but, as he came nearer, he saw that the figure and its attire were surely not hers. He reined up again abruptly, mortified at his disappointment, and a little ashamed lest he should have seemed to have been following an evident stranger. He vaguely remembered, too, that there was a trail to the high road, through a little swale clothed with myrtle and thorn bush which he had just passed, and that she was probably one of his reserved and secluded neighbors—indeed, her dress, in that uncertain light, looked half Spanish. This was more confusing, since his rashness might have been taken for an attempt to force an acquaintance. He wheeled and galloped towards the front of the casa as the figure disappeared at the angle of the wall.

"I don't suppose you ever see any of our neighbors?" said Dick to his aunt casually.

"I really can't say," returned the lady with quiet equanimity. "There were some extraordinary-looking foreigners on the road to San Gregorio yesterday. Manuel, who was driving me, may have known who they were—he is a kind of Indian Papist himself, you know—but I didn't. They might have been relations of his, for all I know."

At any other time Dick would have been amused at this serene relegation of the lofty Estudillos and Peraltas to the caste of the Indian convert, but he was worried to think that perhaps Cecily was really being bored by the absence of neighbors. After dinner, when they sought the rose garden, he dropped upon the little lichen-scarred stone bench by her side. It was still warm from the sun; the hot musk of the roses filled the air; the whole garden, shielded from the cool evening trade winds by its high walls, still kept the glowing memory of the afternoon sunshine. Aunt Viney, with her garden basket on her arm, moved ghost-like among the distant bushes.

"I hope you are not getting bored here?" he said, after a slight inconsequent pause.

"Does that mean that YOU are?" she returned, raising her mischievous eyes to his.

"No; but I thought you might find it lonely, without neighbors."

"I stayed in to-day," she said, femininely replying to the unasked question, "because I fancied Aunt Viney might think it selfish of me to leave her alone so much."

"But YOU are not lonely?"

Certainly not! The young lady was delighted with the whole place, with the quaint old garden, the mysterious corridors, the restful quiet of everything, the picture of dear Aunt Viney—who was just the sweetest soul in the world—moving about like the genius of the casa. It was such a change to all her ideas, she would never forget it. It was so thoughtful of him, Dick, to have given them all that pleasure.

"And the rides," continued Dick, with the untactful pertinacity of the average man at such moments—"you are not tired of THEM?"

No; she thought them lovely. Such freedom and freshness in the exercise; so different from riding in the city or at watering-places, where it was one-half show, and one was always thinking of one's habit or one's self. One quite forgot one's self on that lovely plain—with everything so far away, and only the mountains to look at in the distance. Nevertheless she did not lift her eyes from the point of the little slipper which had strayed beyond her skirt.

Dick was relieved, but not voluble; he could only admiringly follow the curves of her pretty arms and hands, clasped lightly in her lap, down to the point of the little slipper. But even that charming vanishing point was presently withdrawn—possibly through some instinct— for the young lady had apparently not raised her eyes.

"I'm so glad you like it," said Dick earnestly, yet with a nervous hesitation that made his speech seem artificial to his own ears. "You see I—that is—I had an idea that you might like an occasional change of company. It's a great pity we're not on speaking terms with one of these Spanish families. Some of the men, you know, are really fine fellows, with an old-world courtesy that is very charming."

He was surprised to see that she had lifted her head suddenly, with a quick look that however changed to an amused and half coquettish smile.

"I am finding no fault with my present company," she said demurely, dropping her head and eyelids until a faint suffusion seemed to follow the falling lashes over her cheek. "I don't think YOU ought to undervalue it."

If he had only spoken then! The hot scent of the roses hung suspended in the air, which seemed to be hushed around them in mute expectancy; the shadows which were hiding Aunt Viney from view were also closing round the bench where they sat. He was very near her; he had only to reach out his hand to clasp hers, which lay idly in her lap. He felt himself glowing with a strange emanation; he even fancied that she was turning mechanically towards him, as a flower might turn towards the fervent sunlight. But he could not speak; he could scarcely collect his thoughts, conscious though he was of the absurdity of his silence. What was he waiting for? what did he expect? He was not usually bashful, he was no coward; there was nothing in her attitude to make him hesitate to give expression to what he believed was his first real passion. But he could do nothing. He even fancied that his face, turned towards hers, was stiffening into a vacant smile.

The young girl rose. "I think I heard Aunt Viney call me," she said constrainedly, and made a hesitating step forward. The spell which had held Dick seemed to be broken suddenly; he stretched forth his arm to detain her. But the next step appeared to carry her beyond his influence; and it was even with a half movement of rejection that she quickened her pace and disappeared down the path. Dick fell back dejectedly into his seat, yet conscious of a feeling of RELIEF that bewildered him.

But only for a moment. A recollection of the chance that

he had impotently and unaccountably thrown away returned to him. He tried to laugh, albeit with a glowing cheek, over the momentary bashfulness which he thought had overtaken him, and which must have made him ridiculous in her eyes. He even took a few hesitating steps in the direction of the path where she had disappeared. The sound of voices came to his ear, and the light ring of Cecily's laughter. The color deepened a little on his cheek; he re-entered the house and went to his room.

The red sunset, still faintly showing through the heavily recessed windows to the opposite wall, made two luminous aisles through the darkness of the long low apartment. From his easy-chair he watched the color drop out of the sky, the yellow plain grow pallid and seem to stretch itself to infinite rest; then a black line began to deepen and creep towards him from the horizon edge; the day was done. It seemed to him a day lost. He had no doubt now but that he loved his cousin, and the opportunity of telling her so—of profiting by her predisposition of the moment—had passed. She would remember herself, she would remember his weak hesitancy, she would despise him. He rose and walked uneasily up and down. And yet—and it disgusted him with himself still more—he was again conscious of the feeling of relief he had before experienced. A vague formula, "It's better as it is," "Who knows what might have come of it?" he found himself repeating, without reason and without resignation.

Ashamed even of his seclusion, he rose to join the little family circle, which now habitually gathered around a table on the veranda of the patio under the rays of a swinging lamp to take their chocolate. To his surprise the veranda was empty and dark; a light shining from the inner drawing-room showed him his aunt in her armchair reading, alone. A slight thrill ran over him: Cecily might be still in the garden! He noiselessly passed the drawing-room door, turned into a long corridor, and slipped through a grating in the wall into the lane that separated it from the garden. The gate was still open; a few paces brought him into the long alley of roses. Their strong perfume—confined in the high, hot walls—at first made him giddy. This was followed by an inexplicable languor; he turned instinctively towards the stone bench and sank upon it. The long rows of calla lilies against the opposite wall looked ghostlike in the darkness, and seemed to have turned their white faces towards him. Then he fancied that ONE had detached itself from the rank and was moving away. He looked again: surely there was something gliding along the wall! A quick tremor of anticipation passed over him. It was Cecily, who had lingered in the garden—perhaps to give him one more opportunity! He rose quickly, and stepped towards the apparition, which had now plainly resolved itself into a slight girlish figure; it slipped on beneath the trees; he followed quickly—his nervous hesitancy had vanished before what now seemed to be a half-coy, half-coquettish evasion of him. He called softly, "Cecily!" but she did not heed him; he quickened his pace—she increased hers. They were both running. She reached the angle of the wall where the gate opened upon the road. Suddenly she stopped, as if intentionally, in the clear open space before it. He could see her distinctly. The lace mantle slipped from her head and shoulders. It was NOT Cecily!

But it was a face so singularly beautiful and winsome that he was as quickly arrested. It was a woman's deep, passionate eyes and heavy hair, joined to a childish oval of cheek and chin, an infantine mouth, and a little nose whose faintly curved outline redeemed the lower face from weakness and brought it into charming harmony with the rest. A yellow rose was pinned in the lustrous black hair above the little ear; a yellow silk shawl or mantle, which had looked white in the shadows, was thrown over one shoulder and twisted twice or thrice around the plump but petite bust. The large black velvety eyes were fixed on his in half wonderment, half amusement; the lovely lips were parted in half astonishment and half a smile. And yet she was like a picture, a dream,—a materialization of one's most fanciful imaginings,—like anything, in fact, but the palpable flesh and blood she evidently was, standing only a few feet before him, whose hurried breath he could see even now heaving her youthful breast.

His own breath appeared suspended, although his heart beat rapidly as he stammered out: "I beg your pardon—I thought—" He stopped at the recollection that this was the SECOND time he had followed her.

She did not speak, although her parted lips still curved with their faint coy smile. Then she suddenly lifted her right hand, which had been hanging at her side, clasping some long black object like a stick. Without any apparent impulse from her fingers, the stick slowly seemed to broaden in her little hand into the segment of an opening disk, that, lifting to her face and shoulders, gradually eclipsed the upper part of her figure, until, mounting higher, the beautiful eyes and the yellow rose of her hair alone remained above—a large unfurled fan! Then the long eyelashes drooped, as if in a mute farewell, and they too disappeared as the fan was lifted higher. The half-hidden figure appeared to glide to the gateway, lingered for an instant, and vanished. The astounded Dick stepped quickly into the road, but fan and figure were swallowed up in the darkness.

Amazed and bewildered, he stood for a moment, breathless and irresolute. It was no doubt the same stranger that he had seen before. But WHO was she, and what was she doing there? If she were one of their Spanish neighbors, drawn simply by curiosity to become a trespasser, why had she lingered to invite a scrutiny that would clearly identify her? It was not the escapade of that giddy girl which the lower part of her face had suggested, for such a one would have giggled and instantly flown; it was not the deliberate act of a grave woman of the world, for its sequel was so purposeless. Why had she revealed herself to HIM alone? Dick felt himself glowing with a half-shamed, half-secret pleasure. Then he remembered Cecily, and his own purpose in coming into the garden. He hurriedly made a tour of the walks and shrubbery, ostentatiously calling her, yet seeing, as in a dream, only the beautiful eyes of the stranger still before him, and conscious of an ill-defined remorse and disloyalty he had never known before. But Cecily was not there; and again he experienced the old sensation of relief!

He shut the garden gate, crossed the road, and found the grille just closing behind a slim white figure. He started, for it was Cecily; but even in his surprise he was conscious of wondering how he could have ever mistaken the stranger for her. She appeared startled too; she looked pale and abstracted. Could she have been a witness of his strange interview

?Her first sentence dispelled the idea.

"I suppose you were in the garden?" she said, with a certain timidity. "I didn't go there—it seemed so close and stuffy—but walked a little down the lane."

A moment before he would have eagerly told her his

adventure; but in the presence of her manifest embarrassment his own increased. He concluded to tell her another time. He murmured vaguely that he had been looking for her in the garden, yet he had a flushing sense of falsehood in his reserve; and they passed silently along the corridor and entered the patio together. She lit the hanging lamp mechanically. She certainly WAS pale; her slim hand trembled slightly. Suddenly her eyes met his, a faint color came into her cheek, and she smiled. She put up her hand with a girlish gesture towards the back of her head.

"What are you looking at? Is my hair coming down?"

"No," hesitated Dick, "but—I—thought—you were looking just a LITTLE pale."

An aggressive ray slipped into her blue eyes.

"Strange! I thought YOU were. Just now at the grille you looked as if the roses hadn't agreed with you."

They both laughed, a little nervously, and Conchita brought the chocolate. When Aunt Viney came from the drawing-room she found the two young people together, and Cecily in a gale of high spirits.

She had had SUCH a wonderfully interesting walk, all by herself, alone on the plain. It was really so queer and elfish to find one's self where one could see nothing above or around one anywhere but stars. Stars above one, to right and left of one, and some so low down they seemed as if they were picketed on the plain. It was so odd to find the horizon line at one's very feet, like a castaway at sea. And the wind! it seemed to move one this way and that way, for one could not see anything, and might really be floating in the air. Only once she thought she saw something, and was quite frightened.

"What was it?" asked Dick quickly.

"Well, it was a large black object; but—it turned out only to be a horse."

She laughed, although she had evidently noticed her cousin's eagerness, and her own eyes had a nervous brightness.

"And where was Dick all this while?" asked Aunt Viney quietly.

Cecily interrupted, and answered for him briskly. "Oh, he was trying to make attar of rose of himself in the garden. He's still stupefied by his own sweetness."

"If this means," said Aunt Viney, with matter-of-fact precision, "that you've been gallivanting all alone, Cecily, on that common plain, where you're likely to meet all sorts of foreigners and tramps and savages, and Heaven knows what other vermin, I shall set my face against a repetition of it. If you MUST go out, and Dick can't go with you—and I must say that even you and he going out together there at night isn't exactly the kind of American Christian example to set to our neighbors—you had better get Concepcion to go with you and take a lantern."

"But there is nobody one meets on the plain—at least, nobody likely to harm one," protested Cecily.

"Don't tell ME," said Aunt Viney decidedly; "haven't I seen all sorts of queer figures creeping along by the brink after nightfall between San Gregorio and the next rancho? Aren't they always skulking backwards and forwards to mass and aguardiente?"

"And I don't know why WE should set any example to our neighbors. We don't see much of them, or they of us."

"Of course not," returned Aunt Viney; "because all proper Spanish young ladies are shut up behind their grilles at night. You don't see THEM traipsing over the plain in the darkness, WITH or WITHOUT cavaliers! Why, Don Rafael would lock one of HIS sisters up in a convent and consider her disgraced forever, if he heard of it."

Dick felt his cheeks burning; Cecily slightly paled. Yet both said eagerly together: "Why, what do YOU know about it, Aunty?"

"A great deal," returned Aunt Viney quietly, holding her tatting up to the light and examining the stitches with a critical eye. "I've got my eyes about me, thank heaven! even if my ears don't understand the language. And there's a great deal, my dears, that you young people might learn from these Papists."

"And do you mean to say," continued Dick, with a glowing cheek and an uneasy smile, "that Spanish girls don't go out alone?"

"No young LADY goes out without her duenna," said Aunt Viney emphatically. "Of course there's the Concha variety, that go out without even stockings."

As the conversation flagged after this, and the young people once or twice yawned nervously, Aunt Viney thought they had better go to bed.

But Dick did not sleep. The beautiful face beamed out

again from the darkness of his room; the light that glimmered through his deep-set curtainless windows had an odd trick of bringing out certain hanging articles, or pieces of furniture, into a resemblance to a mantled figure. The deep, velvety eyes, fringed with long brown lashes, again looked into his with amused, childlike curiosity. He scouted the harsh criticisms of Aunt Viney, even while he shrank from proving to her her mistake in the quality of his mysterious visitant. Of course she was a lady—far superior to any of her race whom he had yet met. Yet how should he find WHO she was? His pride and a certain chivalry forbade his questioning the servants—before whom it was the rule of the household to avoid all reference to their neighbors. He would make the acquaintance of the old padre—perhaps HE might talk. He would ride early along the trail in the direction of the nearest rancho,—Don Jose Amador's,—a thing he had hitherto studiously refrained from doing. It was three miles away. She must have come that distance, but not ALONE. Doubtless she had kept her duenna in waiting in the road. Perhaps it was she who had frightened Cecily. Had Cecily told ALL she had seen? Her embarrassed manner certainly suggested more than she had told. He felt himself turning hot with an indefinite uneasiness. Then he tried to compose himself. After all, it was a thing of the past. The fair unknown had bribed the duenna for once, no doubt—had satisfied her girlish curiosity—she would not come again! But this thought brought with it such a sudden sense of utter desolation, a deprivation so new and startling, that it frightened him. Was his head turned by the witcheries of some black-eyed schoolgirl whom he had seen but once? Or—he felt his cheeks glowing in the darkness—was it really a case of love at first sight, and she herself had been impelled by the same yearning that now possessed him? A delicious satisfaction followed, that left a smile on his lips as if it had been a kiss. He knew now why he had so strangely hesitated with Cecily. He had never really loved her—he had never known what love was till now!

He was up early the next morning, skimming the plain on the back of "Chu Chu," before the hacienda was stirring. He did not want any one to suspect his destination, and it was even with a sense of guilt that he dashed along the swale in the direction of the Amador rancho. A few vaqueros, an old Digger squaw carrying a basket, two little Indian acolytes on their way to mass passed him. He was surprised to find that there were no ruts of carriage wheels within three miles of the casa, and evidently no track for carriages through the swale. SHE must have come on HORSEBACK. A broader highway, however, intersected the trail at a point where the low walls of the Amador rancho came in view. Here he was startled by the apparition of an old-fashioned family carriage drawn by two large piebald mules. But it was unfortunately closed. Then, with a desperate audacity new to his reserved nature, he ranged close beside it, and even stared in the windows. A heavily mantled old woman, whose brown face was in high contrast to her snow-white hair, sat in the back seat. Beside her was a younger companion, with the odd blonde hair and blue eyes sometimes seen in the higher Castilian type. For an instant the blue eyes caught his, half-coquettishly. But the girl was NOT at all like his mysterious visitor, and he fell, discomfited, behind.

He had determined to explain his trespass on the grounds of his neighbor, if questioned, by the excuse that he was hunting a strayed mustang. But his presence, although watched with a cold reserve by the few peons who were lounging near the gateway, provoked no challenge from them; and he made a circuit of the low adobe walls, with their barred windows and cinnamon-tiled roofs, without molestation—but equally without satisfaction. He felt he was a fool for imagining that he would see her in that way. He turned his horse towards the little Mission half a mile away. There he had once met the old padre, who spoke a picturesque but limited English; now he was only a few yards ahead of him, just turning into the church. The padre was pleased to see Don Ricardo; it was an unusual thing for the Americanos, he observed, to be up so early: for himself, he had his functions, of course. No, the ladies that the caballero had seen had not been to mass! They were Donna Maria and her daughter, going to San Gregorio. They comprised ALL the family at the rancho,—there were none others, unless the caballero, of a possibility, meant Donna Inez, a maiden aunt of sixty— an admirable woman, a saint on earth! He trusted that he would find his estray; there was no doubt a mark upon it, otherwise the plain was illimitable; there were many horses—the world was wide!

Dick turned his face homewards a little less adventurously, and it must be confessed, with a growing sense of his folly. The keen, dry morning air brushed away his fancies of the preceding night; the beautiful eyes that had lured him thither seemed to flicker and be blown out by its practical breath. He began to think remorsefully of his cousin, of his aunt,—of his treachery to that reserve which the little alien household had maintained towards their Spanish neighbors. He found Aunt Viney and Cecily at breakfast—Cecily, he thought, looking a trifle pale. Yet (or was it only his fancy?) she seemed curious about his morning ride. And he became more reticent.

"You must see a good many of our neighbors when you are out so early?"

"Why?" he asked shortly, feeling his color rise.

"Oh, because—because we don't see them at any other time."

"I saw a very nice chap—I think the best of the lot," he began, with assumed jocularity; then, seeing Cecily's eyes suddenly fixed on him, he added, somewhat lamely, "the padre! There were also two women in a queer coach."

"Donna Maria Amador, and Dona Felipa Peralta—her daughter by her first husband," said Aunt Viney quietly. "When you see the horses you think it's a circus; when you look inside the carriage you KNOW it's a funeral."

Aunt Viney did not condescend to explain how she had acquired her genealogical knowledge of her neighbor's family, but succeeded in breaking the restraint between the young people. Dick proposed a ride in the afternoon, which was cheerfully accepted by Cecily. Their intercourse apparently recovered its old frankness and freedom, marred only for a moment when they set out on the plain. Dick, really to forget his preoccupation of the morning, turned his horse's head AWAY from the trail, to ride in another direction; but Cecily oddly, and with an exhibition of caprice quite new to her, insisted upon taking the old trail. Nevertheless they met nothing, and soon became absorbed in the exercise. Dick felt something of his old tenderness return to this wholesome, pretty girl at his side; perhaps he betrayed it in his voice, or in an unconscious lingering by her bridle-rein, but she accepted it with a naive reserve which he naturally attributed to the effect of his own previous preoccupation. He bore it so gently, however, that it awakened her interest, and, possibly, her pique. Her reserve relaxed, and by the time they returned to the hacienda they had regained something of their former intimacy. The dry, incisive breath of the plains swept away the last lingering remnants of yesterday's illusions. Under this frankly open sky, in this clear perspective of the remote Sierras, which admitted no fanciful deception of form or distance—there remained nothing but a strange incident—to be later explained or forgotten. Only he could not bring himself to talk to HER about it.

After dinner, and a decent lingering for coffee on the veranda, Dick rose, and leaning half caressingly, half mischievously, over his aunt's rocking-chair, but with his eyes on Cecily, said:—

"I've been deeply considering, dear Aunty, what you said last evening of the necessity of our offering a good example to our neighbors. Now, although Cecily and I are cousins, yet, as I am HEAD of the house, lord of the manor, and padron, according to the Spanish ideas I am her recognised guardian and protector, and it seems to me it is my positive DUTY to accompany her if she wishes to walk out this evening."

A momentary embarrassment—which, however, changed quickly into an answering smile to her cousin—came over Cecily's face. She turned to her aunt.

"Well, don't go too far," said that lady quietly.

When they closed the grille behind them and stepped into the lane, Cecily shot a quick glance at her cousin.

"Perhaps you'd rather walk in the garden?"

"I? Oh, no," he answered honestly. "But"—he hesitated—"would you?"

"Yes," she said faintly.

He impulsively offered his arm; her slim hand slipped lightly through it and rested on his sleeve. They crossed the lane together, and entered the garden. A load appeared to be lifted from his heart; the moment seemed propitious, —here was a chance to recover his lost ground, to regain his self-respect and perhaps his cousin's affection. By a common instinct, however, they turned to the right, and AWAY from the stone bench, and walked slowly down the broad allee.

They talked naturally and confidingly of the days when they had met before, of old friends they had known and changes that had crept into their young lives; they spoke affectionately of the grim, lonely, but self-contained old woman they had just left, who had brought them thus again together. Cecily talked of Dick's studies, of the scientific work on which he was engaged, that was to bring him, she was sure, fame and fortune! They talked of the thoughtful charm of the old house, of its quaint old-world flavor. They spoke of the beauty of the night, the flowers and the stars, in whispers, as one is apt to do—as fearing to disturb a super-sensitiveness in nature.

They had come out later than on the previous night; and the moon, already risen above the high walls of the garden, seemed a vast silver shield caught in the interlacing tops of the old pear-trees, whose branches crossed its bright field like dark bends or bars. As it rose higher, it began to separate the lighter shrubbery, and open white lanes through the olive-trees. Damp currents of air, alternating with drier heats, on what appeared to be different levels, moved across the whole garden, or gave way at times to a breathless lull and hush of everything, in which the long rose alley seemed to be swooning in its own spices. They had reached the bottom of the garden, and had turned, facing the upper moonlit extremity and the bare stone bench. Cecily's voice faltered, her hand leaned more heavily on his arm, as if she were overcome by the strong perfume. His right hand began to steal towards hers. But she had stopped; she was trembling.

"Go on," she said in a half whisper. "Leave me a moment; I'll join you afterwards."

"You are ill, Cecily! It's those infernal flowers!" said Dick earnestly. "Let me help you to the bench."

"No—it's nothing. Go on, please. Do! Will you go!"

She spoke with imperiousness, unlike herself. He walked on mechanically a dozen paces and turned. She had disappeared. He remembered there was a smaller gate opening upon the plain near where they had stopped. Perhaps she had passed through that. He continued on, slowly, towards the upper end of the garden, occasionally turning to await her return. In this way he gradually approached the stone bench. He was facing about to continue his walk, when his heart seemed to stop beating. The beautiful visitor of last night was sitting alone on the bench before him!

She had not been there a moment before; he could have sworn it. Yet there was no illusion now of shade or distance. She was scarcely six feet from him, in the bright moonlight. The whole of her exquisite little figure was visible, from her lustrous hair down to the tiny, black satin, low-quartered slipper, held as by two toes. Her face was fully revealed; he could see even the few minute freckles, like powdered allspice, that heightened the pale satin sheen of her beautifully rounded cheek; he could detect even the moist shining of her parted red lips, the white outlines of her little teeth, the length of her curved lashes, and the meshes of the black lace veil that fell from the yellow rose above her ear to the black silk camisa; he noted even the thick yellow satin saya, or skirt, heavily flounced with black lace and bugles, and that it was a different dress from that worn on the preceding night, a half-gala costume, carried with the indescribable air of a woman looking her best and pleased to do so: all this he had noted, drawing nearer and nearer, until near enough to forget it all and drown himself in the depths of her beautiful eyes. For they were no longer childlike and wondering: they were glowing with expectancy, anticipation—love!

He threw himself passionately on the bench beside her. Yet, even if he had known her language, he could not have spoken. She leaned towards him; their eyes seemed to meet caressingly, as in an embrace. Her little hand slipped from the yellow folds of her skirt to the bench. He eagerly seized it. A subtle thrill ran through his whole frame. There was no delusion here; it was flesh and blood, warm, quivering, and even tightening round his own. He was about to carry it to his lips, when she rose and stepped backwards. He pressed eagerly forward. Another backward step brought her to the pear-tree, where she seemed to plunge into its shadow. Dick Bracy followed— and the same shadow seemed to fold them in its embrace.

*****

He did not return to the veranda and chocolate that evening, but sent word from his room that he had retired, not feeling well.

Cecily, herself a little nervously exalted, corroborated the fact of his indisposition by telling Aunt Viney that the close odors of the rose garden had affected them both.

Indeed, she had been obliged to leave before him. Perhaps in waiting for her return—and she really was not well enough to go back—he was exposed to the night air too long. She was very sorry.

Aunt Viney heard this with a slight contraction of her brows and a renewed scrutiny of her knitting; and, having satisfied herself by a personal visit to Dick's room that he was not alarmingly ill, set herself to find out what was really the matter with the young people; for there was no doubt that Cecily was in some vague way as disturbed and preoccupied as Dick. He rode out again early the next morning, returning to his studies in the library directly after breakfast; and Cecily was equally reticent, except when, to Aunt Viney's perplexity, she found excuses for Dick's manner on the ground of his absorption in his work, and that he was probably being bored by want of society. She proposed that she should ask an old schoolfellow to visit them.

"It would give Dick a change of ideas, and he would not be perpetually obliged to look so closely after me." She blushed slightly under Aunt Viney's gaze, and added hastily, "I mean, of course, he would not feel it his DUTY."

She even induced her aunt to drive with her to the old mission church, where she displayed a pretty vivacity and interest in the people they met, particularly a few youthful and picturesque caballeros. Aunt Viney smiled gravely. Was the poor child developing an unlooked-for coquetry, or preparing to make the absent-minded Dick jealous? Well, the idea was not a bad one. In the evening she astonished the two cousins by offering to accompany them into the garden—a suggestion accepted with eager and effusive politeness by each, but carried out with great awkwardness by the distrait young people later. Aunt Viney clearly saw that it was not her PRESENCE that was required. In this way two or three days elapsed without apparently bringing the relations of Dick and Cecily to any more satisfactory conclusion. The diplomatic Aunt Viney confessed herself puzzled.

One night it was very warm; the usual trade winds had died away before sunset, leaving an unwonted hush in sky and plain. There was something so portentous in this sudden withdrawal of that rude stimulus to the otherwise monotonous level, that a recurrence of such phenomena was always known as "earthquake weather." The wild cattle moved uneasily in the distance without feeding; herds of unbroken mustangs approached the confines of the hacienda in vague timorous squads. The silence and stagnation of the old house was oppressive, as if the life had really gone out of it at last; and Aunt Viney, after waiting impatiently for the young people to come in to chocolate, rose grimly, set her lips together, and went out into the lane. The gate of the rose garden opposite was open. She walked determinedly forward and entered.

In that doubly stagnant air the odor of the roses was so suffocating and overpowering that she had to stop to take breath. The whole garden, except a near cluster of pear-trees, was brightly illuminated by the moonlight. No one was to be seen along the length of the broad allee, strewn an inch deep with scattered red and yellow petals— colorless in the moonbeams. She was turning away, when Dick's familiar voice, but with a strange accent of entreaty in it, broke the silence. It seemed to her vaguely to come from within the pear-tree shadow.

"But we must understand one another, my darling! Tell me all. This suspense, this mystery, this brief moment of happiness, and these hours of parting and torment, are killing me!"

A slight cough broke from Aunt Viney. She had heard enough—she did not wish to hear more. The mystery was explained. Dick loved Cecily; the coyness or hesitation was not on HIS part. Some idiotic girlish caprice, quite inconsistent with what she had noticed at the mission church, was keeping Cecily silent, reserved, and exasperating to her lover. She would have a talk with the young lady, without revealing the fact that she had overheard them. She was perhaps a little hurt that affairs should have reached this point without some show of confidence to her from the young people. Dick might naturally be reticent—but Cecily!

She did not even look towards the pear-tree, but turned and walked stiffly out of the gate. As she was crossing the lane she suddenly started back in utter dismay and consternation! For Cecily, her niece,—in her own proper person,—was actually just coming OUT OF THE HOUSE!

Aunt Viney caught her wrist. "Where have you been?" she asked quickly.

"In the house," stammered Cecily, with a frightened face.

"You have not been in the garden with Dick?" continued Aunt Viney sharply—yet with a hopeless sense of the impossibility of the suggestion.

"No, I was not even going there. I thought of just strolling down the lane."

The girl's accents were truthful; more than that, she

absolutely looked relieved by her aunt's question. "Do you want me, Aunty?" she added quickly.

"Yes—no. Run away, then—but don't go far."

At any other time Aunt Viney might have wondered at the eagerness with which Cecily tripped away; now she was only anxious to get rid of her. She entered the casa hurriedly.

"Send Josefa to me at once," she said to Manuel.

Josefa, the housekeeper,—a fat Mexican woman,— appeared. "Send Concha and the other maids here." They appeared, mutely wondering. Aunt Viney glanced hurriedly over them—they were all there—a few comely, but not too attractive, and all stupidly complacent. "Have you girls any friends here this evening—or are you expecting any?" she demanded. Of a surety, no!—as the padrona knew—it was not night for church. "Very well," returned Aunt Viney; "I thought I heard your voices in the garden; understand, I want no gallivanting there. Go to bed."

She was relieved! Dick certainly was not guilty of a low intrigue with one of the maids. But who and what was she?

Dick was absent again from chocolate; there was unfinished work to do. Cecily came in later, just as Aunt Viney was beginning to be anxious. Had she appeared distressed or piqued by her cousin's conduct, Aunt Viney might have spoken; but there was a pretty color on her cheek—the result, she said, of her rapid walking, and the fresh air; did Aunt Viney know that a cool breeze had just risen?—and her delicate lips were wreathed at times in a faint retrospective smile. Aunt Viney stared; certainly the girl was not pining! What young people were made of now-a-days she really couldn't conceive. She shrugged her shoulders and resumed her tatting.

Nevertheless, as Dick's unfinished studies seemed to have whitened his cheek and impaired his appetite the next morning, she announced her intention of driving out towards the mission alone. When she returned at luncheon she further astonished the young people by casually informing them they would have Spanish visitors to dinner—namely, their neighbors, Donna Maria Amador and the Dona Felipa Peralta.

Both faces were turned eagerly towards her; both said almost in the same breath, "But, Aunt Viney! you don't know them! However did you—What does it all mean?"

"My dears," said Aunt Viney placidly, "Mrs. Amador and I have always nodded to each other, and I knew they were only waiting for the slightest encouragement. I gave it, and they're coming."

It was difficult to say whether Cecily's or Dick's face betrayed the greater delight and animation. Aunt Viney looked from the one to the other. It seemed as if her attempt at diversion had been successful.

"Tell us all about it, you dear, clever, artful Aunty!" said Cecily gayly.

"There's nothing whatever to tell, my love! It seems, however, that the young one, Dona Felipa, has seen Dick, and remembers him." She shot a keen glance at Dick, but was obliged to admit that the rascal's face remained unchanged. "And I wanted to bring a cavalier for YOU, dear, but Don Jose's nephew isn't at home now." Yet here, to her surprise, Cecily was faintly blushing.

Early in the afternoon the piebald horses and dark brown chariot of the Amadors drew up before the gateway. The young people were delighted with Dona Felipa, and thought her blue eyes and tawny hair gave an added piquancy to her colorless satin skin and otherwise distinctively Spanish face and figure. Aunt Viney, who entertained Donna Maria, was nevertheless watchful of the others; but failed to detect in Dick's effusive greeting, or the Dona's coquettish smile of recognition, any suggestion of previous confidences. It was rather to Cecily that Dona Felipa seemed to be characteristically exuberant and childishly feminine. Both mother and stepdaughter spoke a musical infantine English, which the daughter supplemented with her eyes, her eyebrows, her little brown fingers, her plump shoulders, a dozen charming intonations of voice, and a complete vocabulary in her active and emphatic fan.

The young lady went over the house with Cecily curiously, as if recalling some old memories. "Ah, yes, I remember it—but it was long ago and I was very leetle—you comprehend, and I have not arrive mooch when the old Don was alone. It was too—too—what you call melank-oaly. And the old man have not make mooch to himself of company."

"Then there were no young people in the house, I suppose?" said Cecily, smiling.

"No—not since the old man's father lif. Then there were TWO. It is a good number, this two, eh?" She gave a single gesture, which took in, with Cecily, the distant Dick, and with a whole volume of suggestion in her shoulders, and twirling fan, continued: "Ah! two sometime make one—is it not? But not THEN in the old time—ah, no! It is a sad story. I shall tell it to you some time, but not to HIM."

But Cecily's face betrayed no undue bashful conscious-ness, and she only asked, with a quiet smile, "Why not to—to my cousin?"

"Imbecile!" responded that lively young lady.

After dinner the young people proposed to take Dona Felipa into the rose garden, while Aunt Viney entertained Donna Maria on the veranda. The young girl threw up her hands with an affectation of horror. "Santa Maria!—in the rose garden? After the Angelus, you and him? Have you not heard?"

But here Donna Maria interposed. Ah! Santa Maria! What was all that! Was it not enough to talk old woman's gossip and tell vaqueros tales at home, without making uneasy the strangers? She would have none of it. "Vamos!"

Nevertheless Dona Felipa overcame her horror of the rose garden at infelicitous hours, so far as to permit herself to be conducted by the cousins into it, and to be installed like a rose queen on the stone bench, while Dick and Cecily threw themselves in submissive and imploring attitudes at her little feet. The young girl looked mischievously from one to the other.

"It ees very pret-ty, but all the same I am not a rose: I am what you call a big goose-berry! Eh—is it not?"

The cousins laughed, but without any embarrassed consciousness. "Dona Felipa knows a sad story of this house," said Cecily; "but she will not tell it before you, Dick."

Dick, looking up at the coquettish little figure, with Heaven knows what OTHER memories in his mind, implored and protested.

"Ah! but this little story—she ees not so mooch sad of herself as she ees str-r-r-ange!" She gave an exaggerated little shiver under her lace shawl, and closed her eyes meditatively.

"Go on," said Dick, smiling in spite of his interested expectation.

Dona Felipa took her fan in both hands, spanning her knees, leaned forward, and after a preliminary comp-ressing of her lips and knitting of her brows, said:—

"It was a long time ago. Don Gregorio he have his daughter Rosita here, and for her he will fill all thees rose garden and gif to her; for she like mooch to lif with the rose. She ees very pret-ty. You shall have seen her picture here in the casa. No? It have hang under the crucifix in the corner room, turn around to the wall—WHY, you shall comprehend when I have made finish thees story. Comes to them here one day Don Vincente, Don Gregorio's nephew, to lif when his father die. He was yong, a pollio—same as Rosita. They were mooch together; they have make lofe. What will you?—it ees always the same. The Don Gregorio have comprehend; the friends have all comprehend; in a year they will make marry. Dona Rosita she go to Monterey to see his family. There ees an English warship come there; and Rosita she ees very gay with the officers, and make the flirtation very mooch. Then Don Vincente he is onhappy, and he revenge himself to make lofe with another. When Rosita come back it is very miserable for them both, but they say nossing. The warship he have gone away; the other girl Vincente he go not to no more. All the same, Rosita and Vincente are very triste, and the family will not know what to make. Then Rosita she is sick and eat nossing, and walk to herself all day in the rose garden, until she is as white and fade away as the rose. And Vincente he eat nossing, but drink mooch aguardiente. Then he have fever and go dead. And Rosita she have fainting and fits; and one day they have look for her in the rose garden, and she is not! And they poosh and poosh in the ground for her, and they find her with so mooch rose-leaves—so deep— on top of her. SHE has go dead. It is a very sad story, and when you hear it you are very, very mooch dissatisfied."

It is to be feared that the two Americans were not as thrilled by this sad recital as the fair narrator had expected, and even Dick ventured to point out that those sort of things happened also to his countrymen, and were not peculiar to the casa.

"But you said that there was a terrible sequel," suggested Cecily smilingly: "tell us THAT. Perhaps Mr. Bracy may receive it a little more politely."

An expression of superstitious gravity, half real, half simulated, came over Dona Felipa's face, although her vivacity of gesticulation and emphasis did not relax. She cast a hurried glance around her, and leaned a little forward towards the cousins.

"When there are no more young people in the casa because they are dead," she continued, in a lower voice, "Don Gregorio he is very melank-oaly, and he have no more company for many years. Then there was a rodeo near the hacienda, and there came five or six caballeros to stay with him for the feast. Notabilimente comes then Don Jorge Martinez. He is a bad man—so weeked—a Don Juan for making lofe to the ladies. He lounge in the garden, he smoke his cigarette, he twist the moustache— so! One day he came in, and he laugh and wink so and say, 'Oh, the weeked, sly Don Gregorio! He have hid away in the casa a beautiful, pret-ty girl, and he will nossing say.' And the other caballeros say, 'Mira! what is this? there is not so mooch as one young lady in the casa.' And Don Jorge he wink, and he say, 'Imbeciles! pigs!' And he walk in the garden and twist his moustache more than ever. And one day, behold! he walk into the casa, very white and angry, and he swear mooch to himself; and he orders his horse, and he ride away, and never come back no more, never-r-r! And one day another caballero, Don Esteban Briones, he came in, and say, 'Hola! Don Jorge has forgotten his pret-ty girl: he have left her over on the garden bench. Truly I have seen.' And they say, 'We will too.' And they go, and there is nossing. And they say, 'Imbecile and pig!' But he is not imbecile and pig; for he has seen, and Don Jorge has seen; and why? For it is not a girl, but what you call her—a ghost! And they will that Don Esteban should make a picture of her—a design; and he make one. And old Don Gregorio he say, 'madre de Dios! it is Rosita'—the same that hung under the crucifix in the big room."

"And is that all?" asked Dick, with a somewhat pronounced laugh, but a face that looked quite white in the moonlight.

"No, it ees NOT all. For when Don Gregorio got himself more company another time—it ees all yonge ladies, and my aunt she is invite too; for she was yonge then, and she herself have tell to me this:—

"One night she is in the garden with the other girls, and when they want to go in the casa one have say, 'Where is Francisca Pacheco? Look, she came here with us, and now she is not.' Another one say, 'She have conceal herself to make us affright.' And my aunt she say, 'I will go seek that I shall find her.' And she go. And when she came to the pear-tree, she heard Francisca's voice, and it say to some one she see not, 'Fly! vamos! some one have come.' And then she come at the moment upon Francisca, very white and trembling, and—alone. And Francisca she have run away and say nossing, and shut herself in her room. And one of the other girls say: 'It is the handsome caballero with the little black moustache and sad white face that I have seen in the garden that make this. It is truly that he is some poor relation of Don Gregorio, or some mad kinsman that he will not we should know.' And my aunt ask Don Gregorio; for she is yonge. And he have say: 'What silly fool ees thees? There is not one caballero here, but myself.' And when the other young girl have tell to him how the caballero look, he say: 'The saints save us! I cannot more say. It ees Don Vincente, who haf gone dead.' And he cross himself, and—But look! Madre de Dios! Mees Cecily, you are ill—you are affrighted. I am a gabbling fool! Help her, Don Ricardo; she is falling!"

But it was too late: Cecily had tried to rise to her feet, had staggered forward and fallen in a faint on the bench.

*****

Dick did not remember how he helped to carry the insensible Cecily to the casa, nor what explanation he had given to the alarmed inmates of her sudden attack. He recalled vaguely that something had been said of the overpowering perfumes of the garden at that hour, that the lively Felipa had become half hysterical in her remorseful apologies, and that Aunt Viney had ended the scene by carrying Cecily into her own room, where she presently recovered a still trembling but reticent consciousness. But the fainting of his cousin and the presence of a real emergency had diverted his imagination from the vague terror that had taken possession of it, and for the moment enabled him to control himself. With a desperate effort he managed to keep up a show of hospitable civility to his Spanish friends until their early departure. Then he hurried to his own room. So bewildered and horrified he had become, and a prey to such superstitious terrors, that he could not at that moment bring himself to the test of looking for the picture of the alleged Rosita, which might still be hanging in his aunt's room. If it were really the face of his mysterious visitant—in his present terror—he felt that his reason might not stand the shock. He would look at it to-morrow, when he was calmer! Until then he would believe that the story was some strange coincidence with what must have been his hallucination, or a vulgar trick to which he had fallen a credulous victim. Until then he would believe that Cecily's fright had been only the effect of Dona Felipa's story, acting upon a vivid imagination, and not a terrible confirmation of something she had herself seen. He threw himself, without undressing, upon his bed in a benumbing agony of doubt.

The gentle opening of his door and the slight rustle of a skirt started him to his feet with a feeling of new and overpowering repulsion. But it was a familiar figure that he saw in the long aisle of light which led from his recessed window, whose face was white enough to have been a spirit's, and whose finger was laid upon its pale lips, as it softly closed the door behind it.

"Cecily!"

"Hush!" she said, in a distracted whisper: "I felt I must see you to-night. I could not wait until day—no, not another hour! I could not speak to you before them. I could not go into that dreadful garden again, or beyond the walls of this house. Dick, I want to—I MUST tell you something! I would have kept it from every one—from you most of all! I know you will hate me, and despise me; but, Dick, listen!"—she caught his hand despairingly, drawing it towards her—"that girl's awful story was TRUE!" She threw his hand away.

"And you have seen HER!" said Dick, frantically. "Good God!"

The young girl's manner changed. "HER!" she said, half scornfully, "you don't suppose I believe THAT story? No. I—I—don't blame me, Dick,—I have seen HIM."

"Him?"

She pushed him nervously into a seat, and sat down beside him. In the half light of the moon, despite her pallor and distraction, she was still very human, womanly, and attractive in her disorder.

"Listen to me, Dick. Do you remember one afternoon, when we were riding together, I got ahead of you, and dashed off to the casa. I don't know what possessed me, or WHY I did it. I only know I wanted to get home quickly, and get away from you. No, I was not angry, Dick, at YOU; it did not seem to be THAT; I—well, I confess I was FRIGHTENED—at something, I don't know what. When I wheeled round into the lane, I saw—a man—a young gentleman standing by the garden-wall. He was very picturesque-looking, in his red sash, velvet jacket, and round silver buttons; handsome, but oh, so pale and sad! He looked at me very eagerly, and then suddenly drew back, and I heard you on Chu Chu coming at my heels. You must have seen him and passed him too, I thought: but when you said nothing of it, I—I don't know why, Dick, I said nothing of it too. Don't speak!" she added, with a hurried gesture: "I know NOW why you said nothing,—YOU had not seen him."

She stopped, and put back a wisp of her disordered chestnut hair.

"The next time was the night YOU were so queer, Dick, sitting on that stone bench. When I left you—I thought you didn't care to have me stay—I went to seek Aunt Viney at the bottom of the garden. I was very sad, but suddenly I found myself very gay, talking and laughing with her in a way I could not account for. All at once, looking up, I saw HIM standing by the little gate, looking at me very sadly. I think I would have spoken to Aunt Viney, but he put his finger to his lips—his hand was so slim and white, quite like a hand in one of those Spanish pictures—and moved slowly backwards into the lane, as if he wished to speak with ME only—out there. I know I ought to have spoken to Aunty; I knew it was wrong what I did, but he looked so earnest, so appealing, so awfully sad, Dick, that I slipped past Aunty and went out of the gate. Just then she missed me, and called. He made a kind of despairing gesture, raising his hand Spanish fashion to his lips, as if to say good-night. You'll think me bold, Dick, but I was so anxious to know what it all meant, that I gave a glance behind to see if Aunty was following, before I should go right up to him and demand an explanation. But when I faced round again, he was gone! I walked up and down the lane and out on the plain nearly half an hour, seeking him. It was strange, I know; but I was not a bit FRIGHTENED, Dick—that was so queer—but I was only amazed and curious."

The look of spiritual terror in Dick's face here seemed to give way to a less exalted disturbance, as he fixed his eyes on Cecily's.

"You remember I met YOU coming in: you seemed so queer then that I did not say anything to you, for I thought you would laugh at me, or reproach me for my boldness; and I thought, Dick, that—that—that—this person wished to speak only to ME." She hesitated.

"Go on," said Dick, in a voice that had also undergone a singular change.

The chestnut head was bent a little lower, as the young girl nervously twisted her fingers in her lap.

"Then I saw him again—and—again," she went on hesitatingly. "Of course I spoke to him, to—to—find out what he wanted; but you know, Dick, I cannot speak Spanish, and of course he didn't understand me, and didn't reply."

"But his manner, his appearance, gave you some idea of his meaning?" said Dick suddenly.

Cecily's head drooped a little lower. "I thought—that is, I fancied I knew what he meant."

"No doubt," said Dick, in a voice which, but for the superstitious horror of the situation, might have impressed a casual listener as indicating a trace of human irony.

But Cecily did not seem to notice it. "Perhaps I was excited that night, perhaps I was bolder because I knew you were near me; but I went up to him and touched him!

And then, Dick!—oh, Dick! think how awful—"

Again Dick felt the thrill of superstitious terror creep over him. "And he vanished!" he said hoarsely.

"No—not at once," stammered Cecily, with her head almost buried in her lap; "for he—he—he took me in his arms and—"

"And kissed you?" said Dick, springing to his feet, with every trace of his superstitious agony gone from his indignant face. But Cecily, without raising her head, caught at his gesticulating hand.

"Oh, Dick, Dick! do you think he really did it? The horror of it, Dick! to be kissed by a—a—man who has been dead a hundred years!"

"A hundred fiddlesticks!" said Dick furiously. "We have been deceived! No," he stammered, "I mean YOU have been deceived—insulted!"

"Hush! Aunty will hear you," murmured the girl despairingly.

Dick, who had thrown away his cousin's hand, caught it again, and dragged her along the aisle of light to the window. The moon shone upon his flushed and angry face.

"Listen!" he said; "you have been fooled, tricked— infamously tricked by these people, and some confederate, whom—whom I shall horsewhip if I catch. The whole story is a lie!"

"But you looked as if you believed it—about the girl,"

Bret Harte

said Cecily; "you acted so strangely. I even thought, Dick, —sometimes—you had seen HIM."

Dick shuddered, trembled; but it is to be feared that the lower, more natural human element in him triumphed.

"Nonsense!" he stammered; "the girl was a foolish farrago of absurdities, improbable on the face of things, and impossible to prove. But that infernal, sneaking rascal was flesh and blood."

It seemed to him to relieve the situation and establish his own sanity to combat one illusion with another. Cecily had already been deceived—another lie wouldn't hurt her. But, strangely enough, he was satisfied that Cecily's visitant was real, although he still had doubts about his own.

"Then you think, Dick, it was actually some real man?" she said piteously. "Oh, Dick, I have been so foolish!"

Foolish she no doubt had been; pretty she certainly was, sitting there in her loosened hair, and pathetic, appealing earnestness. Surely the ghostly Rosita's glances were never so pleading as these actual honest eyes behind their curving lashes. Dick felt a strange, new-born sympathy of suffering, mingled tantalizingly with a new doubt and jealousy, that was human and stimulating.

"Oh, Dick, what are WE to do?"

The plural struck him as deliciously sweet and subtle. Had they really been singled out for this strange experience, or still stranger hallucination? His arm crept around her; she gently withdrew from it.

"I must go now," she murmured; "but I couldn't sleep until I told you all. You know, Dick, I have no one else to come to, and it seemed to me that YOU ought to know it first. I feel better for telling you. You will tell me tomorrow what you think we ought to do."

They reached the door, opening it softly. She lingered for a moment on the threshold.

"Tell me, Dick" (she hesitated), "if that—that really were a spirit, and not a real man,—you don't think that—that kiss" (she shuddered) "could do me harm!"

He shuddered too, with a strange and sympathetic consciousness that, happily, she did not even suspect. But he quickly recovered himself and said, with something of bitterness in his voice, "I should be more afraid if it really were a man."

"Oh, thank you, Dick!"

Her lips parted in a smile of relief; the color came faintly back to her cheek.

A wild thought crossed his fancy that seemed an inspiration. They would share the risks alike. He leaned towards her: their lips met in their first kiss.

"Oh, Dick!"

"Dearest!"

"I think—we are saved."

"Why?"

"It wasn't at all like that."

He smiled as she flew swiftly down the corridor. Perhaps he thought so too.

*****

No picture of the alleged Rosita was ever found. Dona Felipa, when the story was again referred to, smiled discreetly, but was apparently too preoccupied with the return of Don Jose's absent nephew for further gossiping visits to the hacienda; and Dick and Cecily, as Mr. and Mrs. Bracy, would seem to have survived—if they never really solved—the mystery of the Hacienda de los Osos. Yet in the month of June, when the moon is high, one does not sit on the stone bench in the rose garden after the last stroke of the Angelus.

CHU CHU

I do not believe that the most enthusiastic lover of that "useful and noble animal," the horse, will claim for him the charm of geniality, humor, or expansive confidence. Any creature who will not look you squarely in the eye—whose only oblique glances are inspired by fear, distrust, or a view to attack; who has no way of returning caresses, and whose favorite expression is one of head-lifting disdain, may be "noble" or "useful," but can be hardly said to add to the gayety of nations. Indeed it may be broadly stated that, with the single exception of gold-fish, of all animals kept for the recreation of mankind the horse is alone capable of exciting a passion that shall be absolutely hopeless. I deem these general remarks necessary to prove that my unreciprocated affection for "Chu Chu" was not purely individual or singular. And I may add that to these general characteristics she brought the waywardness of her capricious sex.

She came to me out of the rolling dust of an emigrant wagon, behind whose tailboard she was gravely trotting. She was a half-broken colt—in which character she had at different times unseated everybody in the train—and, although covered with dust, she had a beautiful coat, and the most lambent gazelle-like eyes I had ever seen. I think she kept these latter organs purely for ornament—

Bret Harte

apparently looking at things with her nose, her sensitive ears, and, sometimes, even a slight lifting of her slim near fore-leg. On our first interview I thought she favored me with a coy glance, but as it was accompanied by an irrelevant "Look out!" from her owner, the teamster, I was not certain. I only know that after some conver-sation, a good deal of mental reservation, and the disbursement of considerable coin, I found myself standing in the dust of the departing emigrant-wagon with one end of a forty-foot riata in my hand, and Chu Chu at the other.

I pulled invitingly at my own end, and even advanced a step or two towards her. She then broke into a long disdainful pace, and began to circle round me at the extreme limit of her tether. I stood admiring her free action for some moments—not always turning with her, which was tiring—until I found that she was gradually winding herself up ON ME! Her frantic astonishment when she suddenly found herself thus brought up against me was one of the most remarkable things I ever saw, and nearly took me off my legs. Then when she had pulled against the riata until her narrow head and prettily arched neck were on a perfectly straight line with it, she as suddenly slackened the tension and condescended to follow me, at an angle of her own choosing. Sometimes it was on one side of me, sometimes on the other. Even then the sense of my dreadful contiguity apparently would come upon her like a fresh discovery, and she would become hysterical. But I do not think that she really SAW me. She looked at the riata and sniffed it disparagingly, she pawed some pebbles that were near me tentatively with her small hoof; she started back with a Robinson Crusoe-like horror of my footprints in the wet gully, but my actual personal presence she ignored. She would sometimes pause, with her head thoughtfully between her fore-legs, and apparently say: "There is some extraordinary presence here: animal, vegetable, or mineral —I can't make out which—but it's not good to eat, and I loathe and detest it."

When I reached my house in the suburbs, before entering the "fifty vara" lot inclosure, I deemed it prudent to leave her outside while I informed the household of my purchase; and with this object I tethered her by the long riata to a solitary sycamore which stood in the centre of the road, the crossing of two frequented thoroughfares. It was not long, however, before I was interrupted by shouts and screams from that vicinity, and on returning thither I found that Chu Chu, with the assistance of her riata, had securely wound up two of my neighbors to the tree, where they presented the appearance of early Christian martyrs. When I released them it appeared that they had been attracted by Chu Chu's graces, and had offered her overtures of affection, to which she had characteristically rotated with this miserable result. I led her, with some difficulty, warily keeping clear of the riata, to the inclosure, from whose fence I had previously removed several bars. Although the space was wide enough to have admitted a troop of cavalry she affected not to notice it, and managed to kick away part of another section on entering. She resisted the stable for some time, but after carefully examining it with her hoofs, and an affectedly meek outstretching of her nose, she consented to recognize some oats in the feed-box—without looking at them—and was formally installed. All this while she had resolutely ignored my presence. As I stood watching her she suddenly stopped eating; the same reflective look came over her. "Surely I am not mistaken, but that same obnoxious creature is somewhere about here!" she seemed to say, and shivered at the possibility.

It was probably this which made me confide my

unreciprocated affection to one of my neighbors—a man supposed to be an authority on horses, and particularly of that wild species to which Chu Chu belonged. It was he who, leaning over the edge of the stall where she was complacently and, as usual, obliviously munching, absolutely dared to toy with a pet lock of hair which she wore over the pretty star on her forehead. "Ye see, captain," he said with jaunty easiness, "hosses is like wimmen; ye don't want ter use any standoffishness or shyness with THEM; a stiddy but keerless sort o' familiarity, a kind o' free but firm handlin', jess like this, to let her see who's master"—

We never clearly knew HOW it happened; but when I picked up my neighbor from the doorway, amid the broken splinters of the stall rail, and a quantity of oats that mysteriously filled his hair and pockets, Chu Chu was found to have faced around the other way, and was contemplating her forelegs, with her hind ones in the other stall. My neighbor spoke of damages while he was in the stall, and of physical coercion when he was out of it again. But here Chu Chu, in some marvelous way, righted herself, and my neighbor departed hurriedly with a brimless hat and an unfinished sentence.

My next intermediary was Enriquez Saltello—a youth of my own age, and the brother of Consuelo Saltello, whom I adored. As a Spanish Californian he was presumed, on account of Chu Chu's half-Spanish origin, to have superior knowledge of her character, and I even vaguely believed that his language and accent would fall familiarly on her ear. There was the drawback, however, that he always preferred to talk in a marvelous English, combining Castilian precision with what he fondly believed to be Californian slang.

"To confer then as to thees horse, which is not—observe me—a Mexican plug! Ah, no! you can your boots bet on that. She is of Castilian stock—believe me and strike me dead! I will myself at different times overlook and affront her in the stable, examine her as to the assault, and why she should do thees thing. When she is of the exercise I will also accost and restrain her. Remain tranquil, my friend! When a few days shall pass much shall be changed, and she will be as another. Trust your oncle to do thees thing! Comprehend me? Everything shall be lovely, and the goose hang high!"

Conformably with this he "overlooked" her the next day, with a cigarette between his yellow-stained finger-tips, which made her sneeze in a silent pantomimic way, and certain Spanish blandishments of speech which she received with more complacency. But I don't think she ever even looked at him. In vain he protested that she was the "dearest" and "littlest" of his "little loves"—in vain he asserted that she was his patron saint, and that it was his soul's delight to pray to her; she accepted the compliment with her eyes fixed upon the manger. When he had exhausted his whole stock of endearing diminutives, adding a few playful and more audacious sallies, she remained with her head down, as if inclined to meditate upon them. This he declared was at least an improvement on her former performances. It may have been my own jealousy, but I fancied she was only saying to herself, "Gracious! can there be TWO of them?"

"Courage and patience, my friend," he said, as we were slowly quitting the stable. "Thees horse is yonge, and has not yet the habitude of the person. To-morrow, at another season, I shall give to her a foundling" ("fondling," I have reason to believe, was the word intended by Enriquez)— "and we shall see. It shall be as easy as to fall away from a log. A leetle more of this chin music which your friend Enriquez possesses, and some tapping of the head and neck, and you are there. You are ever the right side up. Houp la! But let us not precipitate this thing. The more haste, we do not so much accelerate ourselves."

He appeared to be suiting the action to the word as he lingered in the doorway of the stable. "Come on," I said.

"Pardon," he returned, with a bow that was both elaborate and evasive, "but you shall yourself precede me—the stable is YOURS."

"Oh, come along!" I continued impatiently. To my surprise he seemed to dodge back into the stable again. After an instant he reappeared.

"Pardon! but I am re-strain! Of a truth, in this instant I am grasp by the mouth of thees horse in the coat-tail of my dress! She will that I should remain. It would seem"—he disappeared again—"that"—he was out once more—"the experiment is a sooccess! She reciprocate! She is, of a truth, gone on me. It is lofe!"—a stronger pull from Chu Chu here sent him in again—"but"—he was out now triumphantly with half his garment torn away—"I shall coquet."

Nothing daunted, however, the gallant fellow was back next day with a Mexican saddle, and attired in the complete outfit of a vaquero. Overcome though HE was by heavy deerskin trousers, open at the side from the knees down, and fringed with bullion buttons, an enormous flat sombrero, and a stiff, short embroidered velvet jacket, I was more concerned at the ponderous saddle and equipments intended for the slim Chu Chu. That these would hide and conceal her beautiful curves and contour, as well as overweight her, seemed certain; that she would resist them all to the last seemed equally clear. Nevertheless, to my surprise, when she was led out, and the saddle thrown deftly across her back, she was passive. Was it possible that some drop of her old Spanish blood responded to its clinging embrace? She did not either look at it nor smell it. But when Enriquez began to tighten the "cinch" or girth a more singular thing occurred. Chu Chu visibly distended her slender barrel to twice its dimensions; the more he pulled the more she swelled, until I was actually ashamed of her. Not so Enriquez. He smiled at us, and complacently stroked his thin moustache.

"Eet is ever so! She is the child of her grandmother! Even when you shall make saddle thees old Castilian stock, it will make large—it will become a balloon! Eet is a trick—eet is a leetle game—believe me. For why?"

I had not listened, as I was at that moment astonished to see the saddle slowly slide under Chu Chu's belly, and her figure resume, as if by magic, its former slim proportions. Enriquez followed my eyes, lifted his shoulders, shrugged them, and said smilingly, "Ah, you see!"

When the girths were drawn in again with an extra pull or two from the indefatigable Enriquez, I fancied that Chu Chu nevertheless secretly enjoyed it, as her sex is said to appreciate tight-lacing. She drew a deep sigh, possibly of satisfaction, turned her neck, and apparently tried to glance at her own figure—Enriquez promptly with-drawing to enable her to do so easily. Then the dread moment arrived. Enriquez, with his hand on her mane, suddenly paused and, with exaggerated courtesy, lifted his hat and made an inviting gesture.

"You will honor me to precede."

I shook my head laughingly.

"I see," responded Enriquez gravely. "You have to attend the obsequies of your aunt who is dead, at two of the clock. You have to meet your broker who has bought you feefty share of the Comstock lode—at thees moment—or you are loss! You are excuse! Attend! Gentlemen, make your bets! The band has arrived to play! 'Ere we are!"

With a quick movement the alert young fellow had vaulted into the saddle. But, to the astonishment of both of us, the mare remained perfectly still. There was Enriquez bolt upright in the stirrups, completely over-shadowing by his saddle-flaps, leggings, and gigantic spurs the fine proportions of Chu Chu, until she might have been a placid Rosinante, bestridden by some youthful Quixote. She closed her eyes, she was going to sleep! We were dreadfully disappointed. This clearly would not do. Enriquez lifted the reins cautiously! Chu Chu moved forward slowly—then stopped, apparently lost in reflection.

"Affront her on thees side."

I approached her gently. She shot suddenly into the air, coming down again on perfectly stiff legs with a springless jolt. This she instantly followed by a succession of other rocket-like propulsions, utterly unlike a leap, all over the inclosure. The movements of the unfortunate Enriquez were equally unlike any equitation I ever saw. He appeared occasionally over Chu Chu's head, astride of her neck and tail, or in the free air, but never IN the saddle. His rigid legs, however, never lost the stirrups, but came down regularly, accentuating her springless hops. More than that, the disproportionate excess of rider, saddle, and accoutrements was so great that he had, at times, the appearance of lifting Chu Chu forcibly from the ground by superior strength, and of actually contributing to her exercise! As they came towards me, a wild tossing and flying mass of hoofs and spurs, it was not only difficult to distinguish them apart, but to ascertain how much of the jumping was done by Enriquez separately. At last Chu Chu brought matters to a close by making for the low-stretching branches of an oak-tree which stood at the corner of the lot. In a few moments she emerged from it— but without Enriquez.

I found the gallant fellow disengaging himself from the fork of a branch in which he had been firmly wedged, but still smiling and confident, and his cigarette between his teeth. Then for the first time he removed it, and seating himself easily on the branch with his legs dangling down, he blandly waved aside my anxious queries with a gentle reassuring gesture.

"Remain tranquil, my friend. Thees does not count! I have conquer—you observe—for why? I have NEVER for once ARRIVE AT THE GROUND! Consequent she is disappoint! She will ever that I SHOULD! But I have got her when the hair is not long! Your oncle Henry"—with an angelic wink—"is fly! He is ever a bully boy, with the eye of glass! Believe me. Behold! I am here! Big Injin! Whoop!"

He leaped lightly to the ground. Chu Chu, standing watchfully at a little distance, was evidently astonished at his appearance. She threw out her hind hoofs violently, shot up into the air until the stirrups crossed each other high above the saddle, and made for the stable in a succession of rabbit-like bounds—taking the precaution to remove the saddle, on entering, by striking it against the lintel of the door. "You observe," said Enriquez blandly, "she would make that thing of ME. Not having the good occasion, she ees dissatisfied. Where are you now?"

Two or three days afterwards he rode her again with the same result—accepted by him with the same heroic complacency. As we did not, for certain reasons, care to use the open road for this exercise, and as it was impossible to remove the tree, we were obliged to submit to the inevitable. On the following day I mounted her— undergoing the same experience as Enriquez, with the individual sensation of falling from a third-story window on top of a counting-house stool, and the variation of being projected over the fence. When I found that Chu Chu had not accompanied me, I saw Enriquez at my side. "More than ever is become necessary that we should do thees things again," he said gravely, as he assisted me to my feet. "Courage, my noble General! God and Liberty! Once more on to the breach! Charge, Chestare, charge! Come on, Don Stanley! 'Ere we are!"

He helped me none too quickly to catch my seat again, for it apparently had the effect of the turned peg on the enchanted horse in the Arabian Nights, and Chu Chu instantly rose into the air. But she came down this time before the open window of the kitchen, and I alighted easily on the dresser. The indefatigable Enriquez followed me.

"Won't this do?" I asked meekly.

"It ees BETTER—for you arrive NOT on the ground," he said cheerfully; "but you should not once but a thousand times make trial! Ha! Go and win! Nevare die and say so! 'Eave ahead! 'Eave! There you are!"

Luckily, this time I managed to lock the rowels of my long spurs under her girth, and she could not unseat me. She seemed to recognize the fact after one or two plunges, when, to my great surprise, she suddenly sank to the ground and quietly rolled over me. The action disengaged my spurs, but, righting herself without getting up, she turned her beautiful head and absolutely LOOKED at me!—still in the saddle. I felt myself blushing! But the voice of Enriquez was at my side.

"Errise, my friend; you have conquer! It is SHE who has arrive at the ground! YOU are all right. It is done; believe me, it is feenish! No more shall she make thees thing. From thees instant you shall ride her as the cow—as the rail of thees fence—and remain tranquil. For she is a-broke! Ta-ta! Regain your hats, gentlemen! Pass in your checks! It is ovar! How are you now?" He lit a fresh cigarette, put his hands in his pockets, and smiled at me blandly.

For all that, I ventured to point out that the habit of alighting in the fork of a tree, or the disengaging of one's self from the saddle on the ground, was attended with inconvenience, and even ostentatious display. But Enriquez swept the objections away with a single gesture. "It is the PREENCIPAL—the bottom fact—at which you arrive. The next come of himself! Many horse have achieve to mount the rider by the knees, and relinquish after thees same fashion. My grandfather had a barb of thees kind—but she has gone dead, and so have my grandfather. Which is sad and strange! Otherwise I shall make of them both an instant example!"

I ought to have said that although these performances were never actually witnessed by Enriquez's sister—for reasons which he and I thought sufficient—the dear girl displayed the greatest interest in them, and, perhaps aided by our mutually complimentary accounts of each other, looked upon us both as invincible heroes. It is possible also that she over-estimated our success, for she suddenly demanded that I should RIDE Chu Chu to her house, that she might see her. It was not far; by going through a back lane I could avoid the trees which exercised such a fatal fascination for Chu Chu. There was a pleading, child-like entreaty in Consuelo's voice that I could not resist, with a slight flash from her lustrous dark eyes that I did not care to encourage. So I resolved to try it at all hazards.

My equipment for the performance was modeled after Enriquez's previous costume, with the addition of a few fripperies of silver and stamped leather out of compliment to Consuelo, and even with a faint hope that it might appease Chu Chu. SHE certainly looked beautiful in her glittering accoutrements, set off by her jet-black shining coat. With an air of demure abstraction she permitted me to mount her, and even for a hundred yards or so indulged in a mincing maidenly amble that was not without a touch of coquetry. Encouraged by this, I addressed a few terms of endearment to her, and in the exuberance of my youthful enthusiasm I even confided to her my love for Consuelo, and begged her to be "good" and not disgrace herself and me before my Dulcinea. In my foolish trustfulness I was rash enough to add a caress, and to pat her soft neck. She stopped instantly with a hysteric shudder. I knew what was passing through her mind: she had suddenly become aware of my baleful existence.

The saddle and bridle Chu Chu was becoming accustomed to, but who was this living, breathing object that had actually touched her? Presently her oblique vision was attracted by the fluttering movement of a fallen oak-leaf in the road before her. She had probably seen many oak-leaves many times before; her ancestors had no doubt been familiar with them on the trackless hills and in field and paddock, but this did not alter her profound conviction that I and the leaf were identical, that our baleful touch was something indissolubly connected. She reared before that innocent leaf, she revolved round it, and then fled from it at the top of her speed.

The lane passed before the rear wall of Saltello's garden. Unfortunately, at the angle of the fence stood a beautiful Madrono-tree, brilliant with its scarlet berries, and endeared to me as Consuelo's favorite haunt, under whose protecting shade I had more than once avowed my youthful passion. By the irony of fate Chu Chu caught sight of it, and with a succession of spirited bounds instantly made for it. In another moment I was beneath it, and Chu Chu shot like a rocket into the air. I had barely time to withdraw my feet from the stirrups, to throw up one arm to protect my glazed sombrero and grasp an overhanging branch with the other, before Chu Chu darted off. But to my consternation, as I gained a secure perch on the tree, and looked about me, I saw her— instead of running away—quietly trot through the open gate into Saltello's garden.

Need I say that it was to the beneficent Enriquez that I again owed my salvation? Scarcely a moment elapsed before his bland voice rose in a concentrated whisper from the corner of the garden below me. He had divined the dreadful truth!

"For the love of God, collect to yourself many kinds of thees berry! All you can! Your full arms round! Rest tranquil. Leave to your ole oncle to make for you a delicate exposure. At the instant!"

He was gone again. I gathered, wonderingly, a few of the larger clusters of parti-colored fruit and patiently waited. Presently he reappeared, and with him the lovely Consuelo—her dear eyes filled with an adorable anxiety.

"Yes," continued Enriquez to his sister, with a confidential lowering of tone but great distinctness of utterance, "it is ever so with the American! He will ever make FIRST the salutation of the flower or the fruit, picked to himself by his own hand, to the lady where he call. It is the custom of the American hidalgo! My God—what will you? I make it not—it is so! Without doubt he is in this instant doing thees thing. That is why he have let go his horse to precede him here; it is always the etiquette to offer these things on the feet. Ah! Behold! it is he!—Don Francisco! Even now he will descend from thees tree! Ah! You make the blush, little sister (archly)! I will retire! I am discreet; two is not company for the one! I make tracks! I am gone!"

How far Consuelo entirely believed and trusted her ingenious brother I do not know, nor even then cared to inquire. For there was a pretty mantling of her olive cheek, as I came forward with my offering, and a certain significant shyness in her manner that were enough to throw me into a state of hopeless imbecility. And I was always miserably conscious that Consuelo possessed an exalted sentimentality, and a predilection for the highest mediaeval romance, in which I knew I was lamentably deficient. Even in our most confidential moments I was always aware that I weakly lagged behind this daughter of a gloomily distinguished ancestry, in her frequent incursions into a vague but poetic past. There was something of the dignity of the Spanish chatelaine in the sweetly grave little figure that advanced to accept my specious offering. I think I should have fallen on my knees to present it, but for the presence of the all seeing Enriquez. But why did I even at that moment remember that he had early bestowed upon her the nickname of "Pomposa"? This, as Enriquez himself might have observed, was "sad and strange."

I managed to stammer out something about the Madrono berries being at her "disposicion" (the tree was in her own garden!), and she took the branches in her little brown hand with a soft response to my unutterable glances.

But here Chu Chu, momentarily forgotten, executed a happy diversion. To our astonishment she gravely walked up to Consuelo and, stretching out her long slim neck, not only sniffed curiously at the berries, but even protruded a black underlip towards the young girl herself. In another instant Consuelo's dignity melted. Throwing her arms around Chu Chu's neck she embraced and kissed her. Young as I was, I understood the divine significance of a girl's vicarious effusiveness at such a moment, and felt delighted. But I was the more astonished that the usually sensitive horse not only submitted to these caresses, but actually responded to the extent of affecting to nip my mistress's little right ear.

This was enough for the impulsive Consuelo. She ran hastily into the house, and in a few moments reappeared in a bewitching riding-skirt gathered round her jimp waist. In vain Enriquez and myself joined in earnest entreaty: the horse was hardly broken for even a man's riding yet; the saints alone could tell what the nervous creature might do with a woman's skirt flapping at her side! We begged for delay, for reflection, for at least time to change the saddle—but with no avail! Consuelo was determined, indignant, distressingly reproachful! Ah, well! if Don Pancho (an ingenious diminutive of my

Christian name) valued his horse so highly—if he were jealous of the evident devotion of the animal to herself, he would—but here I succumbed! And then I had the felicity of holding that little foot for one brief moment in the hollow of my hand, of readjusting the skirt as she threw her knee over the saddle-horn, of clasping her tightly— only half in fear—as I surrendered the reins to her grasp. And to tell the truth, as Enriquez and I fell back, although I had insisted upon still keeping hold of the end of the riata, it was a picture to admire. The petite figure of the young girl, and the graceful folds of her skirt, admirably harmonized with Chu Chu's lithe contour, and as the mare arched her slim neck and raised her slender head under the pressure of the reins, it was so like the lifted velvet-capped toreador crest of Consuelo herself, that they seemed of one race.

"I would not that you should hold the riata," said Consuelo petulantly.

I hesitated—Chu Chu looked certainly very amiable—I let go. She began to amble towards the gate, not mincingly as before, but with a freer and fuller stride. In spite of the incongruous saddle the young girl's seat was admirable. As they neared the gate she cast a single mischievous glance at me, jerked at the rein, and Chu Chu sprang into the road at a rapid canter. I watched them fearfully and breathlessly, until at the end of the lane I saw Consuelo rein in slightly, wheel easily, and come flying back. There was no doubt about it; the horse was under perfect control. Her second subjugation was complete and final!

Overjoyed and bewildered, I overwhelmed them with congratulations; Enriquez alone retaining the usual brotherly attitude of criticism, and a superior toleration of a lover's enthusiasm. I ventured to hint to Consuelo (in what I believed was a safe whisper) that Chu Chu only showed my own feelings towards her. "Without doubt," responded Enriquez gravely. "She have of herself assist you to climb to the tree to pull to yourself the berry for my sister." But I felt Consuelo's little hand return my pressure, and I forgave and even pitied him.

From that day forward, Chu Chu and Consuelo were not only firm friends but daily companions. In my devotion I would have presented the horse to the young girl, but with flattering delicacy she preferred to call it mine. "I shall erride it for you, Pancho," she said; "I shall feel," she continued with exalted although somewhat vague poetry, "that it is of YOU! You lofe the beast—it is therefore of a necessity YOU, my Pancho! It is YOUR soul I shall erride like the wings of the wind—your lofe in this beast shall be my only cavalier for ever." I would have preferred something whose vicarious qualities were less uncertain than I still felt Chu Chu's to be, but I kissed the girl's hand submissively. It was only when I attempted to accompany her in the flesh, on another horse, that I felt the full truth of my instinctive fears. Chu Chu would not permit any one to approach her mistress's side. My mounted presence revived in her all her old blind astonishment and disbelief in my existence; she would start suddenly, face about, and back away from me in utter amazement as if I had been only recently created, or with an affected modesty as if I had been just guilty of some grave indecorum towards her sex which she really could not stand. The frequency of these exhibitions in the public highway were not only distressing to me as a simple escort, but as it had the effect on the casual spectators of making Consuelo seem to participate in Chu Chu's objections, I felt that, as a lover, it could not be borne. Any attempt to coerce Chu Chu ended in her running away. And my frantic pursuit of her was open to equal misconstruction. "Go it, Miss, the little dude is gainin' on you!" shouted by a drunken teamster to the frightened Consuelo, once checked me in mid career. Even the dear girl herself saw the uselessness of my real presence, and after a while was content to ride with "my soul."

Notwithstanding this, I am not ashamed to say that it was my custom, whenever she rode out, to keep a slinking and distant surveillance of Chu Chu on another horse, until she had fairly settled down to her pace. A little nod of Consuelo's round black-and-red toreador hat or a kiss tossed from her riding-whip was reward enough!

I remember a pleasant afternoon when I was thus awaiting her in the outskirts of the village. The eternal smile of the Californian summer had begun to waver and grow less fixed; dust lay thick on leaf and blade; the dry hills were clothed in russet leather; the trade winds were shifting to the south with an ominous warm humidity; a few days longer and the rains would be here. It so chanced that this afternoon my seclusion on the roadside was accidentally invaded by a village belle—a Western young lady somewhat older than myself, and of flirtatious reputation. As she persistently and—as I now have reason to believe—mischievously lingered, I had only a passing glimpse of Consuelo riding past at an unaccustomed speed which surprised me at the moment. But as I reasoned later that she was only trying to avoid a merely formal meeting, I thought no more about it. It was not until I called at the house to fetch Chu Chu at the usual hour, and found that Consuelo had not yet returned, that a recollection of Chu Chu's furious pace again troubled me. An hour passed—it was getting towards sunset, but there were no signs of Chu Chu nor her mistress. I became seriously alarmed. I did not care to reveal my fears to the family, for I felt myself responsible for Chu Chu. At last I desperately saddled my horse, and galloped off in the direction she had taken. It was the road to Rosario and the hacienda of one of her relations, where she sometimes halted.

The road was a very unfrequented one, twisting like a mountain river; indeed, it was the bed of an old water-course, between brown hills of wild oats, and debouching at last into a broad blue lake-like expanse of alfalfa meadows. In vain I strained my eyes over the monotonous level; nothing appeared to rise above or move across it. In the faint hope that she might have lingered at the hacienda, I was spurring on again when I heard a slight splashing on my left. I looked around. A broad patch of fresher-colored herbage and a cluster of dwarfed alders indicated a hidden spring. I cautiously approached its quaggy edges, when I was shocked by what appeared to be a sudden vision! Mid-leg deep in the centre of a greenish pool stood Chu Chu! But without a strap or buckle of harness upon her—as naked as when she was foaled!

For a moment I could only stare at her in bewildered terror. Far from recognizing me, she seemed to be absorbed in a nymph-like contemplation of her own graces in the pool. Then I called "Consuelo!" and galloped frantically around the spring. But there was no response, nor was there anything to be seen but the all-unconscious Chu Chu. The pool, thank Heaven! was not deep enough to have drowned any one; there were no signs of a struggle on its quaggy edges. The horse might have come from a distance! I galloped on, still calling. A few hundred yards further I detected the vivid glow of Chu Chu's scarlet saddle-blanket, in the brush near the trail. My heart leaped—I was on the track. I called again; this time a faint reply, in accents I knew too well, came from the field beside me!

Consuelo was there! reclining beside a manzanita bush which screened her from the road, in what struck me, even at that supreme moment, as a judicious and picturesquely selected couch of scented Indian grass and dry tussocks. The velvet hat with its balls of scarlet plush was laid carefully aside; her lovely blue-black hair retained its tight coils undisheveled, her eyes were luminous and tender. Shocked as I was at her apparent helplessness, I remember being impressed with the fact that it gave so little indication of violent usage or disaster.

I threw myself frantically on the ground beside her.

"You are hurt, Consita! For Heaven's sake, what has happened?"

She pushed my hat back with her little hand, and tumbled my hair gently.

"Nothing. YOU are here, Pancho—eet is enofe! What shall come after thees—when I am perhaps gone among the grave—make nothing! YOU are here—I am happy. For a little, perhaps—not mooch."

"But," I went on desperately, "was it an accident? Were you thrown? Was it Chu Chu?"—for somehow, in spite of her languid posture and voice, I could not, even in my fears, believe her seriously hurt.

"Beat not the poor beast, Pancho. It is not from HER comes thees thing. She have make nothing—believe me! I have come upon your assignation with Miss Essmith! I make but to pass you—to fly—to never come back! I have say to Chu Chu, 'Fly!' We fly many miles. Sometimes together, sometimes not so mooch! Sometimes in the saddle, sometimes on the neck! Many things remain in the road; at the end, I myself remain! I have say, 'Courage, Pancho will come!' Then I say, 'No, he is talk with Miss Essmith!' I remember not more. I have creep here on the hands. Eet is feenish!"

I looked at her distractedly. She smiled tenderly, and slightly smoothed down and rearranged a fold of her dress to cover her delicate little boot.

"But," I protested, "you are not much hurt, dearest. You have broken no bones. Perhaps," I added, looking at the boot, "only a slight sprain. Let me carry you to my horse; I will walk beside you, home. Do, dearest Consita!"

She turned her lovely eyes towards me sadly. "You comprehend not, my poor Pancho! It is not of the foot, the ankle, the arm, or the head that I can say, 'She is broke!' I would it were even so. But"—she lifted her sweet lashes slowly—"I have derrange my inside. It is an affair of my family. My grandfather have once toomble over the bull at a rodeo. He speak no more; he is dead. For why? He has derrange his inside. Believe me, it is of the family. You comprehend? The Saltellos are not as the other peoples for this. When I am gone, you will bring to me the berry to grow upon my tomb, Pancho; the berry you have picked for me. The little flower will come too, the little star will arrive, but Consuelo, who lofe you, she will come not more! When you are happy and talk in the road to the Essmith, you will not think of me. You will not see my eyes, Pancho; thees little grass"—she ran her plump little fingers through a tussock—"will hide them; and the small animals in the black coats that lif here will have much sorrow—but you will not. It ees better so! My father will not that I, a Catholique, should marry into a camp-meeting, and lif in a tent, and make howl like the coyote." (It was one of Consuelo's bewildering beliefs that there was only one form of dissent—Methodism!) "He will not that I should marry a man who possess not the many horses, ox, and cow, like him. But I care not. YOU are my only religion, Pancho! I have enofe of the horse, and ox, and cow when YOU are with me! Kiss me, Pancho. Perhaps it is for the last time—the feenish! Who knows?"

There were tears in her lovely eyes; I felt that my own were growing dim; the sun was sinking over the dreary plain to the slow rising of the wind; an infinite loneliness had fallen upon us, and yet I was miserably conscious of some dreadful unreality in it all. A desire to laugh, which I felt must be hysterical, was creeping over me; I dared not speak. But her dear head was on my shoulder, and the situation was not unpleasant.

Nevertheless, something must be done! This was the more difficult as it was by no means clear what had already been done. Even while I supported her drooping figure I was straining my eyes across her shoulder for succor of some kind. Suddenly the figure of a rapid rider appeared upon the road. It seemed familiar. I looked again—it was the blessed Enriquez! A sense of deep relief came over me. I loved Consuelo; but never before had lover ever hailed the irruption of one of his beloved's family with such complacency.

"You are safe, dearest; it is Enriquez!"

I thought she received the information coldly. Suddenly she turned upon me her eyes, now bright and glittering.

"Swear to me at the instant, Pancho, that you will not again look upon Miss Essmith, even for once."

I was simple and literal. Miss Smith was my nearest neighbor, and, unless I was stricken with blindness, compliance was impossible. I hesitated—but swore.

"Enofe—you have hesitate—I will no more."

She rose to her feet with grave deliberation. For an instant, with the recollection of the delicate internal organization of the Saltellos on my mind, I was in agony lest she should totter and fall, even then, yielding up her gentle spirit on the spot. But when I looked again she had a hairpin between her white teeth, and was carefully adjusting her toreador hat. And beside us was Enriquez—cheerful, alert, voluble, and undaunted.

"Eureka! I have found! We are all here! Eet is a leetle public—eh! a leetle too much of a front seat for a tete-a-tete, my yonge friends," he said, glancing at the remains of Consuelo's bower, "but for the accounting of taste there is none. What will you? The meat of the one man shall envenom the meat of the other. But" (in a whisper to me) "as to thees horse—thees Chu Chu, which I have just pass—why is she undress? Surely you would not make an exposition of her to the traveler to suspect! And if not, why so?"

I tried to explain, looking at Consuelo, that Chu Chu had run away, that Consuelo had met with a terrible accident, had been thrown, and I feared had suffered serious internal injury. But to my embarrassment Consuelo maintained a half scornful silence, and an inconsistent freshness of healthful indifference, as Enriquez approached her with an engaging smile. "Ah, yes, she have the headache, and the molligrubs. She will sit on the damp stone when the gentle dew is falling. I comprehend. Meet me in the lane when the clock strike nine! But," in a lower voice, "of thees undress horse I comprehend nothing! Look you—it is sad and strange."

He went off to fetch Chu Chu, leaving me and Consuelo alone. I do not think I ever felt so utterly abject and bewildered before in my life. Without knowing why, I was miserably conscious of having in some way offended the girl for whom I believed I would have given my life, and I had made her and myself ridiculous in the eyes of her brother. I had again failed in my slower Western nature to understand her high romantic Spanish soul! Meantime she was smoothing out her riding-habit, and looking as fresh and pretty as when she first left her house.

"Consita," I said hesitatingly, "you are not angry with me?"

"Angry?" she repeated haughtily, without looking at me. "Oh, no! Of a possibility eet is Mees Essmith who is angry that I have interroopt her tete-a-tete with you, and have send here my brother to make the same with me."

"But," I said eagerly, "Miss Smith does not even know Enriquez!"

Consuelo turned on me a glance of unutterable significance. "Ah!" she said darkly, "you TINK!"

Indeed I KNEW. But here I believed I understood Consuelo, and was relieved. I even ventured to say gently, "And you are better?"

She drew herself up to her full height, which was not much. "Of my health, what is it? A nothing. Yes! Of my soul let us not speak."

Nevertheless, when Enriquez appeared with Chu Chu she ran towards her with outstretched arms. Chu Chu protruded about six inches of upper lip in response— apparently under the impression, which I could quite understand, that her mistress was edible. And, I may have been mistaken, but their beautiful eyes met in an absolute and distinct glance of intelligence!

During the home journey Consuelo recovered her spirits, and parted from me with a magnanimous and forgiving pressure of the hand. I do not know what explanation of Chu Chu's original escapade was given to Enriquez and the rest of the family; the inscrutable forgiveness extended to me by Consuelo precluded any further inquiry on my part. I was willing to leave it a secret between her and Chu Chu. But, strange to say, it seemed to complete our own understanding, and precipitated, not only our lovemaking, but the final catastrophe which culminated that romance. For we had resolved to elope. I do not know that this heroic remedy was absolutely necessary from the attitude of either Consuelo's family or my own; I am inclined to think we preferred it, because it involved no previous explanation or advice. Need I say that our confidant and firm ally was Consuelo's brother—the alert, the linguistic, the ever-happy, ever-ready Enriquez! It was understood that his presence would not only give a certain mature respectability to our performance—but I do not think we would have contemplated this step without it. During one of our riding excursions we were to secure the services of a Methodist minister in the adjoining county, and, later, that of the Mission padre—when the secret was out. "I will gif her away," said Enriquez confidently, "it will on the instant propitiate the old shadbelly who shall perform the affair, and withhold his jaw. A little chin-music from your oncle 'Arry shall finish it! Remain tranquil and forgot not a ring! One does not always, in the agony and dissatisfaction of the moment, a ring remember. I shall bring two in the pocket of my dress."

If I did not entirely participate in this roseate view it may have been because Enriquez, although a few years my senior, was much younger-looking, and with his demure deviltry of eye, and his upper lip close shaven for this occasion, he suggested a depraved acolyte rather than a responsible member of a family. Consuelo had also confided to me that her father—possibly owing to some rumors of our previous escapade—had forbidden any further excursions with me alone. The innocent man did not know that Chu Chu had forbidden it also, and that even on this momentous occasion both Enriquez and myself were obliged to ride in opposite fields like out flankers. But we nevertheless felt the full guilt of disobedience added to our desperate enterprise. Mean-while, although pressed for time, and subject to discovery at any moment, I managed at certain points of the road to dismount and walk beside Chu Chu (who did not seem to recognize me on foot), holding Consuelo's hand in my own, with the discreet Enriquez leading my horse in the distant field. I retain a very vivid picture of that walk—the ascent of a gentle slope towards a prospect as yet unknown, but full of glorious possibilities; the tender dropping light of an autumn sky, slightly filmed with the promise of the future rains, like foreshadowed tears, and the half frightened, half serious talk into which Consuelo and I had insensibly fallen. And then, I don't know how it happened, but as we reached the summit Chu Chu suddenly reared, wheeled, and the next moment was flying back along the road we had just traveled, at the top of her speed! It might have been that, after her abstracted fashion, she only at that moment detected my presence; but so sudden and complete was her evolution that before I could regain my horse from the astonished Enriquez she was already a quarter of a mile on the homeward stretch, with the frantic Consuelo pulling hopelessly at the bridle. We started in pursuit. But a horrible despair seized us. To attempt to overtake her, to even follow at the same rate of speed would only excite Chu Chu and endanger Consuelo's life. There was absolutely no help for it, nothing could be done; the mare had taken her determined long, continuous stride, the road was a straight, steady descent all the way back to the village, Chu Chu had the bit between her teeth, and there was no prospect of swerving her. We could only follow hopelessly, idiotically, furiously, until Chu Chu dashed triumphantly into the Saltellos' courtyard, carrying the half-fainting Consuelo back to the arms of her assembled and astonished family.

It was our last ride together. It was the last I ever saw of Consuelo before her transfer to the safe seclusion of a convent in Southern California. It was the last I ever saw of Chu Chu, who in the confusion of that rencontre was overlooked in her half-loosed harness, and allowed to escape though the back gate to the fields. Months afterwards it was said that she had been identified among a band of wild horses in the Coast Range, as a strange and beautiful creature who had escaped the brand of the rodeo and had become a myth. There was another legend that she had been seen, sleek, fat, and gorgeously caparisoned, issuing from the gateway of the Rosario patio, before a lumbering Spanish cabriole in which a short, stout matron was seated—but I will have none of it. For there are days when she still lives, and I can see her plainly still climbing the gentle slope towards the summit, with

Consuelo on her back, and myself at her side, pressing eagerly forward towards the illimitable prospect that opens in the distance.

MY FIRST BOOK

When I say that my "First Book" was NOT my own, and contained beyond the title-page not one word of my own composition, I trust that I will not be accused of trifling with paradox, or tardily unbosoming myself of youthful plagiary. But the fact remains that in priority of publication the first book for which I became responsible, and which probably provoked more criticism than anything I have written since, was a small compilation of Californian poems indited by other hands.

A well-known bookseller of San Francisco one day handed me a collection of certain poems which had already appeared in Pacific Coast magazines and newspapers, with the request that I should, if possible, secure further additions to them, and then make a selection of those which I considered the most notable and characteristic, for a single volume to be issued by him. I have reason to believe that this unfortunate man was actutated by a laudable desire to publish a pretty Californian book—HIS first essay in publication—and at the same time to foster Eastern immigration by an exhibit of the Californian literary product; but, looking back upon his venture, I am inclined to think that the little volume never contained anything more poetically pathetic or touchingly imaginative than that gentle conception.

Equally simple and trustful was his selection of myself as compiler. It was based somewhat, I think, upon the fact that "the artless Helicon" I boasted "was Youth," but I imagine it was chiefly owing to the circumstance that I had from the outset, with precocious foresight, confided to him my intention of not putting any of my own verses in the volume. Publishers are appreciative; and a self-abnegation so sublime, to say nothing of its security, was not without its effect.

We settled to our work with fatuous self-complacency, and no suspicion of the trouble in store for us, or the storm that was to presently hurtle around our devoted heads. I winnowed the poems, and he exploited a preliminary announcement to an eager and waiting press, and we moved together unwittingly to our doom. I remember to have been early struck with the quantity of material coming in—evidently the result of some popular misunderstanding of the announcement. I found myself in daily and hourly receipt of sere and yellow fragments, originally torn from some dead and gone newspaper, creased and seamed from long folding in wallet or pocketbook. Need I say that most of them were of an emotional or didactic nature; need I add any criticism of these homely souvenirs, often discolored by the morning coffee, the evening tobacco, or, heaven knows! perhaps blotted by too easy tears! Enough that I knew now what had become of those original but never recopied verses which filled the "Poet's Corner" of every country news-paper on the coast. I knew now the genesis of every didactic verse that "coldly furnished forth the marriage table" in the announcement of weddings in the rural press. I knew now who had read—and possibly indited—the dreary hic jacets of the dead in their mourning columns. I knew now why certain letters of the alphabet had been more tenderly considered than others, and affectionately addressed. I knew the meaning of the "Lines to Her who can best understand them," and I knew that they HAD been understood. The morning's post buried my table beneath these withered leaves of posthumous passion. They lay there like the pathetic nosegays of quickly fading wild flowers, gathered by school children, inconsistently abandoned upon roadsides, or as inconsistently treasured as limp and flabby superstitions in their desks. The chill wind from the Bay blowing in at the window seemed to rustle them into sad articulate appeal. I remember that when one of them was whisked from the window by a stronger gust than usual, and was attaining a circulation it had never known before, I ran a block or two to recover it. I was young then, and in an exalted sense of editorial responsibility which I have since survived, I think I turned pale at the thought that the reputation of some unknown genius might have thus been swept out and swallowed by the all-absorbing sea.

There were other difficulties arising from this unexpected wealth of material. There were dozens of poems on the same subject. "The Golden Gate," "Mount Shasta," "The Yosemite," were especially provocative. A beautiful bird known as the "Californian Canary" appeared to have been shot at and winged by every poet from Portland to San Diego. Lines to the "Mariposa" flower were as thick as the lovely blossoms themselves in the Merced valley, and the Madrone tree was as "berhymed" as Rosalind. Again, by a liberal construction of the publisher's announcement, MANUSCRIPT poems, which had never known print, began to coyly unfold their virgin blossoms in the morning's mail. They were accompanied by a few lines stating, casually, that their sender had found them lying forgotten in his desk, or, mendaciously, that they were "thrown off" on the spur of the moment a few hours before. Some of the names appended to them astonished me. Grave, practical business men, sage financiers, fierce speculators, and plodding traders, never before suspected of poetry, or even correct prose, were among the contributors. It seemed as if most of the able-bodied inhabitants of the Pacific Coast had been in the habit at some time of expressing themselves in verse. Some sought confidential interviews with the editor. The climax was reached when, in Montgomery Street, one day, I was approached by a well known and venerable judicial magnate. After some serious preliminary conversation, the old gentleman finally alluded to what he was pleased to call a task of "great delicacy and responsibility laid upon my young shoulders." "In fact," he went on paternally, adding the weight of his judicial hand to that burden, "I have thought of speaking to you about it. In my leisure moments on the Bench I have, from time to time, polished and perfected a certain college poem begun years ago, but which may now be said to have been finished in California, and thus embraced in the scope of your proposed selection. If a few extracts, selected by myself, to save you all trouble and responsibility, be of any benefit to you, my dear young friend, consider them at your service."

In this fashion the contributions had increased to three times the bulk of the original collection, and the difficulties of selection were augmented in proportion. The editor and publisher eyed each other aghast. "Never thought there were so many of the blamed things alive," said the latter with great simplicity, "had you?" The editor had not. "Couldn't you sorter shake 'em up and condense 'em, you know? keep their ideas—and their names— separate, so that they'd have proper credit. See?" The editor pointed out that this would infringe the rule he had laid down. "I see," said the publisher thoughtfully; "well, couldn't you pare 'em down; give the first verse entire and sorter sample the others?" The editor thought not. There was clearly nothing to do but to make a more rigid selection—a difficult performance when the material was uniformly on a certain dead level, which it is not necessary to define here. Among the rejections were, of course, the usual plagiarisms from well-known authors imposed upon an inexperienced country press; several admirable pieces detected as acrostics of patent medicines, and certain veiled libels and indecencies such as mark the "first" publications on blank walls and fences of the average youth. Still the bulk remained too large, and the youthful editor set to work reducing it still more with a sympathizing concern which the good-natured, but unliterary, publisher failed to understand, and which, alas! proved to be equally unappreciated by the rejected contributors.

The book appeared—a pretty little volume typographically, and externally a credit to pioneer book-making. Copies were liberally supplied to the press, and authors and publishers self-complacently awaited the result. To the latter this should have been satisfactory; the book sold readily from his well-known counters to purchasers who seemed to be drawn by a singular curiosity, unaccompanied, however, by any critical comment. People would lounge in to the shop, turn over the leaves of other volumes, say carelessly, "Got a new book of California poetry out, haven't you?" purchase it, and quietly depart. There were as yet no notices from the press; the big dailies were silent; there was something ominous in this calm.

Out of it the bolt fell. A well-known mining weekly, which I here poetically veil under the title of the Red Dog "Jay Hawk," was first to swoop down upon the tuneful and unsuspecting quarry. At this century-end of fastidious and complaisant criticism, it may be interesting to recall the direct style of the Californian "sixties." "The hogwash and 'purp'-stuff ladled out from the slop-bucket of Messrs. —and Co., of 'Frisco, by some lop-eared Eastern apprentice, and called 'A Compilation of Californian Verse,' might be passed over, so far as criticism goes. A club in the hands of any able-bodied citizen of Red Dog, and a steamboat ticket to the Bay, cheerfully contributed from this office, would be all-sufficient. But when an imported greenhorn dares to call his flapdoodle mixture 'Californian,' it is an insult to the State that has produced the gifted 'Yellow Hammer,' whose lofty flights have from time to time dazzled our readers in the columns of the 'Jay Hawk.' That this complacent editorial jackass, browsing among the dock and thistles which he has served up in this volume, should make no allusion to California's greatest bard, is rather a confession of his idiocy than a slur upon the genius of our esteemed contributor." I turned hurriedly to my pile of rejected contributions—the nom de plume of "Yellow Hammer" did NOT appear among them; certainly I had never heard of its existence. Later, when a friend showed me one of that gifted bard's pieces, I was inwardly relieved! It was so like the majority of the other verses, in and out of the volume, that the mysterious poet might have written under a hundred aliases. But the Dutch Flat "Clarion," following, with no uncertain sound, left me small time for consideration. "We doubt," said that journal, "if a more feeble collection of drivel could have been made, even if taken exclusively from the editor's own verses, which we note he has, by an equal editorial incompetency, left out of the volume. When we add that, by a felicity of idiotic selection, this person has chosen only one, and the least characteristic, of the really clever poems of Adoniram Skaggs, which have so often graced these columns, we have said enough to satisfy our readers." The Mormon

Hill "Quartz Crusher" relieved this simple directness with more fancy: "We don't know why Messrs.—and Co. send us, under the title of 'Selections of Californian Poetry,' a quantity of slumgullion which really belongs to the sluices of a placer mining camp, or the ditches of the rural districts. We have sometimes been compelled to run a lot of tailings through our stamps, but never of the grade of the samples offered, which, we should say, would average about 33-1/3 cents per ton. We have, however, come across a single specimen of pure gold evidently overlooked by the serene ass who has compiled this volume. We copy it with pleasure, as it has already shone in the 'Poet's Corner' of the 'Crusher' as the gifted effusion of the talented Manager of the Excelsior Mill, otherwise known to our delighted readers as 'Outcrop.'" The Green Springs "Arcadian" was no less fanciful in imagery: "Messrs.—and Co. send us a gaudy green-and-yellow, parrot-colored volume, which is supposed to contain the first callow 'cheepings' and 'peepings' of Californian songsters. From the flavor of the specimens before us we should say that the nest had been disturbed prematurely. There seems to be a good deal of the parrot inside as well as outside the covers, and we congratulate our own sweet singer 'Blue Bird,' who has so often made these columns melodious, that she has escaped the ignominy of being exhibited in Messrs.—and Co.'s aviary." I should add that this simile of the aviary and its occupants was ominous, for my tuneful choir was relentlessly slaughtered; the bottom of the cage was strewn with feathers! The big dailies collected the criticisms and published them in their own columns with the grim irony of exaggerated head-lines. The book sold tremendously on account of this abuse, but I am afraid that the public was disappointed. The fun and interest lay in the criticisms, and not in any pointedly ludicrous quality in the rather commonplace collection, and I fear I cannot claim for it even that merit.

And it will be observed that the animus of the criticism appeared to be the omission rather than the retention of certain writers.

But this brings me to the most extraordinary feature of this singular demonstration. I do not think that the publishers were at all troubled by it; I cannot conscientiously say that I was; I have every reason to believe that the poets themselves, in and out of the volume, were not displeased at the notoriety they had not expected, and I have long since been convinced that my most remorseless critics were not in earnest, but were obeying some sudden impulse started by the first attacking journal. The extravagance of the Red Dog "Jay Hawk" was emulated by others: it was a large, contagious joke, passed from journal to journal in a peculiar cyclonic Western fashion. And there still lingers, not unpleasantly, in my memory the conclusion of a cheerfully scathing review of the book which may make my meaning clearer: "If we have said anything in this article which might cause a single pang to the poetically sensitive nature of the youthful individual calling himself Mr. Francis Bret Harte—but who, we believe, occasionally parts his name and his hair in the middle—we will feel that we have not labored in vain, and are ready to sing Nunc Dimittis, and hand in our checks. We have no doubt of the absolutely pellucid and lacteal purity of Franky's intentions. He means well to the Pacific Coast, and we return the compliment. But he has strayed away from his parents and guardians while he was too fresh. He will not keep without a little salt."

It was thirty years ago. The book and its Rabelaisian criticisms have been long since forgotten. Alas! I fear that even the capacity for that Gargantuan laughter which met them, in those days, exists no longer. The names I have used are necessarily fictitious, but where I have been obliged to quote the criticisms from memory I have, I believe, only softened their asperity. I do not know that this story has any moral. The criticisms here recorded never hurt a reputation nor repressed a single honest aspiration. A few contributors to the volume, who were of original merit, have made their mark, independently of it or its critics. The editor, who was for two months the most abused man on the Pacific slope, within the year became the editor of its first successful magazine. Even the publisher prospered, and died respected!

ABOUT THE AUTHOR

 **Francis Bret Harte** (August 25, 1836–May 6, 1902) was an American author and poet, best remembered for his accounts of pioneering life in California.

Born in Albany, New York, Harte moved to California in 1853, later working there in a number of capacities, including miner, teacher, messenger, and journalist. He spent part of his life in the northern California coast town now known as Arcata, at the time it was just a mining camp on Humboldt Bay.

His first literary efforts, including poetry and prose, appeared in The Californian, an early literary journal edited by Charles Henry Webb. In 1868 he became editor of The Overland Monthly, another new literary magazine, but this one more in tune with the pioneering spirit of excitement in California. His story, "The Luck of Roaring Camp," appeared in the magazine's second edition, propelling Harte to nationwide fame.

As an established literary figure, he was appointed to the position of United States Consul in the town of Krefeld, Germany in 1878 and Glasgow in 1880. In 1885 he settled in London. During the thirty years he spent in Europe, he never abandoned writing, and maintained a prodigious output of stories that retained the freshness of his earlier work. He died in England in 1902.

Choose from Thousands of 1stWorldLibrary Classics By

A. M. Barnard
Ada Leverson
Adolphus William Ward
Aesop
Agatha Christie
Alexander Aaronsohn
Alexander Kielland
Alexandre Dumas
Alfred Gatty
Alfred Ollivant
Alice Duer Miller
Alice Turner Curtis
Alice Dunbar
Allen Chapman
Alleyne Ireland
Ambrose Bierce
Amelia E. Barr
Amory H. Bradford
Andrew Lang
Andrew McFarland Davis
Andy Adams
Angela Brazil
Anna Alice Chapin
Anna Sewell
Annie Besant
Annie Hamilton Donnell
Annie Payson Call
Annie Roe Carr
Annonaymous
Anton Chekhov
Archibald Lee Fletcher
Arnold Bennett
Arthur C. Benson
Arthur Conan Doyle
Arthur M. Winfield
Arthur Ransome
Arthur Schnitzler
Arthur Train
Atticus
B.H. Baden-Powell
B. M. Bower
B. C. Chatterjee
Baroness Emmuska Orczy
Baroness Orczy
Basil King
Bayard Taylor
Ben Macomber
Bertha Muzzy Bower
Bjornstjerne Bjornson

Booth Tarkington
Boyd Cable
Bram Stoker
C. Collodi
C. E. Orr
C. M. Ingleby
Carolyn Wells
Catherine Parr Traill
Charles A. Eastman
Charles Amory Beach
Charles Dickens
Charles Dudley Warner
Charles Farrar Browne
Charles Ives
Charles Kingsley
Charles Klein
Charles Hanson Towne
Charles Lathrop Pack
Charles Romyn Dake
Charles Whibley
Charles Willing Beale
Charlotte M. Braeme
Charlotte M. Yonge
Charlotte Perkins Stetson
Clair W. Hayes
Clarence Day Jr.
Clarence E. Mulford
Clemence Housman
Confucius
Coningsby Dawson
Cornelis DeWitt Wilcox
Cyril Burleigh
D. H. Lawrence
Daniel Defoe
David Garnett
Dinah Craik
Don Carlos Janes
Donald Keyhoe
Dorothy Kilner
Dougan Clark
Douglas Fairbanks
E. Nesbit
E. P. Roe
E. Phillips Oppenheim
E. S. Brooks
Earl Barnes
Edgar Rice Burroughs
Edith Van Dyne
Edith Wharton

Edward Everett Hale
Edward J. O'Biren
Edward S. Ellis
Edwin L. Arnold
Eleanor Atkins
Eleanor Hallowell Abbott
Eliot Gregory
Elizabeth Gaskell
Elizabeth McCracken
Elizabeth Von Arnim
Ellem Key
Emerson Hough
Emilie F. Carlen
Emily Bronte
Emily Dickinson
Enid Bagnold
Enilor Macartney Lane
Erasmus W. Jones
Ernie Howard Pie
Ethel May Dell
Ethel Turner
Ethel Watts Mumford
Eugene Sue
Eugenie Foa
Eugene Wood
Eustace Hale Ball
Evelyn Everett-green
Everard Cotes
F. H. Cheley
F. J. Cross
F. Marion Crawford
Fannie E. Newberry
Federick Austin Ogg
Ferdinand Ossendowski
Fergus Hume
Florence A. Kilpatrick
Fremont B. Deering
Francis Bacon
Francis Darwin
Frances Hodgson Burnett
Frances Parkinson Keyes
Frank Gee Patchin
Frank Harris
Frank Jewett Mather
Frank L. Packard
Frank V. Webster
Frederic Stewart Isham
Frederick Trevor Hill
Frederick Winslow Taylor

Friedrich Kerst
Friedrich Nietzsche
Fyodor Dostoyevsky
G.A. Henty
G.K. Chesterton
Gabrielle E. Jackson
Garrett P. Serviss
Gaston Leroux
George A. Warren
George Ade
Geroge Bernard Shaw
George Cary Eggleston
George Durston
George Ebers
George Eliot
George Gissing
George MacDonald
George Meredith
George Orwell
George Sylvester Viereck
George Tucker
George W. Cable
George Wharton James
Gertrude Atherton
Gordon Casserly
Grace E. King
Grace Gallatin
Grace Greenwood
Grant Allen
Guillermo A. Sherwell
Gulielma Zollinger
Gustav Flaubert
H. A. Cody
H. B. Irving
H.C. Bailey
H. G. Wells
H. H. Munro
H. Irving Hancock
H. R. Naylor
H. Rider Haggard
H. W. C. Davis
Haldeman Julius
Hall Caine
Hamilton Wright Mabie
Hans Christian Andersen
Harold Avery
Harold McGrath
Harriet Beecher Stowe
Harry Castlemon
Harry Coghill
Harry Houidini

Hayden Carruth
Helent Hunt Jackson
Helen Nicolay
Hendrik Conscience
Hendy David Thoreau
Henri Barbusse
Henrik Ibsen
Henry Adams
Henry Ford
Henry Frost
Henry James
Henry Jones Ford
Henry Seton Merriman
Henry W Longfellow
Herbert A. Giles
Herbert Carter
Herbert N. Casson
Herman Hesse
Hildegard G. Frey
Homer
Honore De Balzac
Horace B. Day
Horace Walpole
Horatio Alger Jr.
Howard Pyle
Howard R. Garis
Hugh Lofting
Hugh Walpole
Humphry Ward
Ian Maclaren
Inez Haynes Gillmore
Irving Bacheller
Isabel Cecilia Williams
Isabel Hornibrook
Israel Abrahams
Ivan Turgenev
J.G.Austin
J. Henri Fabre
J. M. Barrie
J. M. Walsh
J. Macdonald Oxley
J. R. Miller
J. S. Fletcher
J. S. Knowles
J. Storer Clouston
J. W. Duffield
Jack London
Jacob Abbott
James Allen
James Andrews
James Baldwin

James Branch Cabell
James DeMille
James Joyce
James Lane Allen
James Lane Allen
James Oliver Curwood
James Oppenheim
James Otis
James R. Driscoll
Jane Abbott
Jane Austen
Jane L. Stewart
Janet Aldridge
Jens Peter Jacobsen
Jerome K. Jerome
Jessie Graham Flower
John Buchan
John Burroughs
John Cournos
John F. Kennedy
John Gay
John Glasworthy
John Habberton
John Joy Bell
John Kendrick Bangs
John Milton
John Philip Sousa
John Taintor Foote
Jonas Lauritz Idemil Lie
Jonathan Swift
Joseph A. Altsheler
Joseph Carey
Joseph Conrad
Joseph E. Badger Jr
Joseph Hergesheimer
Joseph Jacobs
Jules Vernes
Julian Hawthrone
Julie A Lippmann
Justin Huntly McCarthy
Kakuzo Okakura
Karle Wilson Baker
Kate Chopin
Kenneth Grahame
Kenneth McGaffey
Kate Langley Bosher
Kate Langley Bosher
Katherine Cecil Thurston
Katherine Stokes
L. A. Abbot
L. T. Meade

L. Frank Baum
Latta Griswold
Laura Dent Crane
Laura Lee Hope
Laurence Housman
Lawrence Beasley
Leo Tolstoy
Leonid Andreyev
Lewis Carroll
Lewis Sperry Chafer
Lilian Bell
Lloyd Osbourne
Louis Hughes
Louis Joseph Vance
Louis Tracy
Louisa May Alcott
Lucy Fitch Perkins
Lucy Maud Montgomery
Luther Benson
Lydia Miller Middleton
Lyndon Orr
M. Corvus
M. H. Adams
Margaret E. Sangster
Margret Howth
Margaret Vandercook
Margaret W. Hungerford
Margret Penrose
Maria Edgeworth
Maria Thompson Daviess
Mariano Azuela
Marion Polk Angellotti
Mark Overton
Mark Twain
Mary Austin
Mary Catherine Crowley
Mary Cole
Mary Hastings Bradley
Mary Roberts Rinehart
Mary Rowlandson
M. Wollstonecraft Shelley
Maud Lindsay
Max Beerbohm
Myra Kelly
Nathaniel Hawthrone
Nicolo Machiavelli
O. F. Walton
Oscar Wilde

Owen Johnson
P.G. Wodehouse
Paul and Mabel Thorne
Paul G. Tomlinson
Paul Severing
Percy Brebner
Percy Keese Fitzhugh
Peter B. Kyne
Plato
Quincy Allen
R. Derby Holmes
R. L. Stevenson
R. S. Ball
Rabindranath Tagore
Rahul Alvares
Ralph Bonehill
Ralph Henry Barbour
Ralph Victor
Ralph Waldo Emmerson
Rene Descartes
Ray Cummings
Rex Beach
Rex E. Beach
Richard Harding Davis
Richard Jefferies
Richard Le Gallienne
Robert Barr
Robert Frost
Robert Gordon Anderson
Robert L. Drake
Robert Lansing
Robert Lynd
Robert Michael Ballantyne
Robert W. Chambers
Rosa Nouchette Carey
Rudyard Kipling
Saint Augustine
Samuel B. Allison
Samuel Hopkins Adams
Sarah Bernhardt
Sarah C. Hallowell
Selma Lagerlof
Sherwood Anderson
Sigmund Freud
Standish O'Grady
Stanley Weyman
Stella Benson
Stella M. Francis

Stephen Crane
Stewart Edward White
Stijn Streuvels
Swami Abhedananda
Swami Parmananda
T. S. Ackland
T. S. Arthur
The Princess Der Ling
Thomas A. Janvier
Thomas A Kempis
Thomas Anderton
Thomas Bailey Aldrich
Thomas Bulfinch
Thomas De Quincey
Thomas Dixon
Thomas H. Huxley
Thomas Hardy
Thomas More
Thornton W. Burgess
U. S. Grant
Upton Sinclair
Valentine Williams
Various Authors
Vaughan Kester
Victor Appleton
Victor G. Durham
Victoria Cross
Virginia Woolf
Wadsworth Camp
Walter Camp
Walter Scott
Washington Irving
Wilbur Lawton
Wilkie Collins
Willa Cather
Willard F. Baker
William Dean Howells
William le Queux
W. Makepeace Thackeray
William W. Walter
William Shakespeare
Winston Churchill
Yei Theodora Ozaki
Yogi Ramacharaka
Young E. Allison
Zane Grey